REDEMPTION

BORIS CHRONICLES™ BOOK FOUR

PAUL C. MIDDLETON

MICHAEL ANDERLE

DISRUPTIVE IMAGINATION

LMBPN Publishing
PMB 196, 2540 South Maryland Pkwy
Las Vegas, NV 89109

First US edition, January 2018
Version 1.04, March 2021
Print ISBN: 978-1-64202-961-1

PROLOGUE

Danislav was angry with his boss. Boris shouldn't have decided that now was the time to push the borders of his domain out farther. He sure as hell didn't need to send an old hand like Danislav on one of the first clearance patrols.

Damn that alliance proposal. It had pushed Boris to expand west before the signatory dates, to increase the territory that he would hold in what would become a land grab.

There were gasps from the patrol as suddenly a pillar of smoke appeared on the horizon. There must be a homestead or village in that direction.

He could smell the fear radiating from his patrol. Most people were sensible enough to leave Boris's domain and its borderlands alone, and they were barely ten clicks from the previously established border. It was concerning that people were attacking each other this close to the homeland It was hardly something to be afraid of for an old hand like him, though.

He barked out several orders, and he shifted with three of the others in the platoon. The rest were to follow as quickly as possible behind the scouting Shifters after distributing the gear that those four could no longer carry.

His anger increased at the wanton damage he found in the village that had been set alight. The only undamaged buildings in the hamlet were the inn and the town hall, which neighbored each other and were made of stone with slate roofs. It would be nearly impossible to burn them quickly, unlike the other thatch-roofed buildings.

What concerned him most was the scorch marks from a weapon that he didn't recognize, combined with the smell of Vampire in the air. He hadn't smelt Vampire since the first years after the World's Worst Day Ever.

As he moved closer to the town hall, there were bodies scattered across the street. Many were burnt to a crisp, and only one or two had the telltale bite marks of a Vampire, despite the stench of them being everywhere. He couldn't smell the more rancid odor of Nosferatu, but that was more of a relief to him.

It was unlikely that any Vampires older than the fifth generation were lurking around on Boris's border. Not after the proclamation killing a pair of third gens had made, having thought they could move in on his territory. He'd sent messengers from their forces with eight body parts to travel from village to village in the surrounding lands.

'Really, Boris should be sending his eldest on these patrols,' Danislav thought. Unlike his siblings, Olaf was overprotected by modern standards. For example, his sister, Fiona, was Boris's ambassador to the Mongolians. *'Besides, Olaf is better suited to lead patrols against possible Vampires than I am. I'm just not a Bear, and he is. Sure, I can probably take one in a pinch with backup, but it wouldn't be a fun tangle,'* his thoughts continued.

"Search the town," he ordered. "Look for survivors and look for any information to be had. Regroup at the town hall. Town hall is the operations center."

Once he was inside the building, he reflexively started rearranging furniture to make it as defensible as possible. His mind focused on the other problems he faced. He hoped the rest of the patrol hauled ass to the town. Even with the extra gear, they shouldn't take much longer than an hour.

Starting to look around for any form of records, Danislav couldn't find anything recent other than some town votes. As this place was recovering from the Fall, they had decided on a direct democratic model. He could understand the whys of that, having lived in the practicable autocracy of the Soviet Union. Not that what he saw as the corrupt oligarchy of both Russia and the United States immediately preceding the Fall had been any better to live under.

In fact, the gentle tyranny that Boris imposed was the most pleasant political structure he'd ever been a citizen of. Danislav wanted to keep that authority intact. To do that, the heir, Olaf, needed to be respected, and he needed to find a way to accomplish that.

Rather than being spoiled, Olaf was overprotected. He was a good kid, always trying to please his father and live up to his father's reputation. That was a big part of the problem. Boris's reputation had a damned long shadow now.

It had been hard being the Bear-Lord's adopted son at a time where his reputation was only impressive. Danislav had managed to survive it, but that had come at a cost. He never saw himself as a leader. Not an overall leader, at least.

Lead a unit? Organize a hunting or search party? Danislav could handle that. But to have an entire people's fate in his hands? That was beyond him.

Even knowing that, he suspected that was precisely what Olaf desired. He was also smart enough to know that Boris was the better man for the job in Arkhangelsk Palden.

It didn't help that Boris never let Olaf go further than the inner patrol circuit. Olaf was nearing fifty, but he'd never even visited many of the outer farms. He led inner circuit patrols as often as he could, and no one ever complained about his professionalism or performance, though no one ever complimented them either.

Danislav's journey through that long-worn track of thought was abruptly ended by the entrance of most of the patrol into the town hall. After sending his two best marksmen to the roof with a spotter, he sent five to the inn, to look for food or any supplies that might be useful in fortifying the town hall for the night.

That left him with twenty-two men in his platoon-strength force. Danislav kept two with him to continue strengthening the town hall with what was on hand. He sent the remainder out with a half-dozen digital cameras to find out what the other Shifters might have located as well as finding anything else that might be of interest to document. Lilith could download them when they got back to New Romanovka.

This was hardly the first time one of the extended patrols had run up against an atrocity.

In the fifty years since the Fall, they had developed their own procedure. If they ever ended up tracking down perpetrators? Those perpetrators would end up being executed after a judicial and fair trial with the collected evidence.

Deciding to call in the shuttles was the next concern. While Lilith was a genius when it came to manipulating biology, she was far less capable when it came to physical and mechanical technologies. She could maintain their communication links and devices, but had not managed to replicate what TOM had achieved with the shuttlecraft. Nor did they have the capability to make use of the theory she knew.

To be entirely fair, she didn't have the industrial base to work with. TOM had access to far more when the shuttles were originally built. She had no access to a replicating unit of the size required for many of the major components of that craft.

The squad returned to him from next door. They were carrying a barrel along with as many benches as their combined strength allowed. There was a small selection of hammers, saws, and a drill balanced on one of the benches.

The barrel was half full of triangular iron spikes. They'd make a good substitute for nails and would allow them to shape firing ports into the cut up benches. The benches could then be fastened into the window frames. Once he got a fire burning, the wooden firing embrasures and the remaining shutters should keep the room warm. There was plenty of firewood available, either loose from the half-burnt buildings or in the chopped stack behind the inn.

What amazed Danislav most was when reports from his exploring troopers came in. So many supplies had been left. If they'd been raiders, they'd been particularly incompetent, as most of the cellars were still full of foodstuffs. If it weren't for the fact that the buildings were burnt to the ground, five hundred people could move into the town tomorrow. With the available supplies, they could expect to survive all but the absolute worst a Russian winter could throw at them.

Boris may yet decide to man it as an armed outpost.

Unfortunately, that led to a more significant question. Since the possibility it had been raiders was unlikely, considering how much was left behind, why was so much damage done to the town?

Why kill everyone in a town that was not only surviving in these times, but prospering?

Danislav could only think of two answers, and he didn't like either one. The first reason was that this was a demonstration of force. Being so close to Boris's border, a response would have to be sent after it.

The second was worse.

The final reason Danislav could think of for such wanton slaughter was that the town had been used to test a new weapon. From the level of damage, it could only be a weapon based on alien technology that was somehow modified and advanced after the Fall.

For years, Danislav had desperately hoped that interesting times were over for him. Looking at the damage along with the rape and destruction of this town, it seemed they were not.

Grabbing his communicator, he called in a full report to Boris and Lilith.

CHAPTER ONE

Boris stood in the conference room with Janna sitting calmly in front of him at the table. Danislav's report indicated a problem, but more than that—Lilith and some of his other advisors were at his back about Olaf. He needed a task, or he'd be seen as untrusted and untrustworthy.

They said the protectiveness Janna and he had displayed was seen as distrust—either in his loyalty or his abilities. Janna and Boris had just had the biggest fight of their marriage. She had agreed with the concerned members of the council, if somewhat reluctantly.

So, Boris had called his adopted son in to ask for an honest opinion. He'd been hoping Danislav would have an uneventful patrol. Instead, Danislav had left two-thirds of his unit holding a ravaged village. Two platoons had been sent under a captain to consolidate the position and start constructing some winter barracks over the ruins. Preparations were being made to house two full companies under a major in order to secure and patrol from the site and region.

They would be digging in bunkers, making it able to expand into an administrative center over the coming years. Meanwhile, those companies were to aggressively patrol the local area. If this was a weapons test, it could originate some distance from the base.

The Vampire Danislav had scented was the key to that. Forsaken could be brave enough in a stand-up fight, but they were cautious when unsure of having the greater force. Many would have traveled long distances to test something like this weapon. Even some of Michael's children had acted that way.

The salvaged town would be a useful place to expand his territory from. With the growing population, more land would be needed soon.

That was why he had started sending out the extended range patrols, after all. Arkhangelsk Palden would be the core district of a larger realm.

Still, it was a complication Boris did not need right now. It had taken twenty-five years to reorganize his forces into a mostly 'square' organization. Although the tactical flexibility of three squad platoons had been retained, the rest of the force structure was four companies to a battalion, four battalions to a regiment, and a planned four regiments to the planned Arkhangelsk Palden Division.

Two full-time regiments, two reserves. 'Square' military organizations were simply better for the defense of held land and for slow expansion. It also allowed each regiment to maintain support units.

Many of the smaller settlements in the area had formed local militias that were sent to train under his commanders. There were also other various 'independent' militias that had formed to demonstrate an objection to some of his policies. Each type of militia could field roughly two regiments.

Even the independent militias were considered in his planning. Just because they disliked some of his policies did not mean they refused to answer a callup.

With the destruction of industry that accompanied the

world's worst day ever, Infantry was the only force that made good sense. So, it made sense to integrate light artillery which consisted of mule transported mortars mostly, with a few newly built, horse-drawn, light howitzers and World War One style field guns.

His officer pool was light, however. It would remain so for at least another few years as they completed the build-up and reorganization of the held lands. Already there were diplomats from Finland, Sweden, and the relatively intact Baltic states of Estonia and Latvia asking for defensive alliances against the warlords between what the outer world was calling 'the lands of the Bear Lord' and their territories.

To the west of his lands lay the area they wanted help to stabilize. This new threat was coming from the South-west, with an emphasis on the *south*.

Boris just didn't have the troops to spare. He also feared Danislav's likely solution. He loved his son and wanted to save him from the danger he had experienced in his own life. More, he viewed the risk through the eyes of someone who had served a Tzar, as well as considered how the Tzars had protected their heirs.

In this new world, Lilith had pointed out, there was no way to prevent a person being exposed to the endemic violence.

Finally, Danislav arrived. He was clean and in fresh clothes. Boris couldn't begrudge him the time to shower, change, and probably grab a hot meal. Not after more than a month in the field.

"Lilith has brought me up to date, Boris." Danislav refused to have Lilith 'plug him into' the etheric communications network. There were speakers she could access in the barracks, though. Every officer's room had three, and despite objections over the placement of the third, one of those were in the bathroom.

"You need to send Olaf. He needs to prove himself," Danislav stated, leaving no room for discussion on that point.

"Fuck your mother, Danislav. It's too hard. He doesn't have the training for it." Danislav and Janna snorted at that explosion from Boris.

"I never knew her, Father!" Danislav fired back. Sighing, he continued. "The problem isn't a lack of training, Boris. The problem is *all he has* is the training. He has too little experience backing it up." Anger flashed in Boris's eyes, but for the first time in decades, Danislav simply caught the gaze without backing down.

Finally, the truth of his words, combined with the anger, washed past the oldest son of his heart and wore down the old bear. Guilt replaced passion, and he collapsed into the chair at the head of the conference table.

Scrubbing his face, with fear in his eyes and sorrow in his expression, Boris was silent for a time. When he finally spoke up, his tone was one of self-reproach. He said, "You are right. You've been right for years, probably decades." His voice was that of a broken man when he continued, "But what can I do about it now?"

Janna looked concerned because she had discussed the options with Lilith previously. With the amount of the population that disapproved of the situation, half-measures wouldn't be enough.

Lilith presented her analysis. Over sixty percent of the population disliked Olaf for a variety of reasons, while less than five percent liked him. There was an interesting aspect as to the makeup of the five percent.

Then she went forth with the proposed solution. "We recruit from the self-proclaimed militias in the west and south to form a battalion. Pull some of the most experienced Non-Coms from the regulars to give them a leavening of real military experience and put Olaf in command. Many of those militias object to the restrictions you placed on his movements and command opportunities." She had used the common slang for Non-Commissioned officers or NCOs.

She snorted, "They can hardly object to being placed under his command. They will be a dog's breakfast, but all those we're talking about have completed the year of military service you require."

Boris went pale as a sheet, but nodded slowly. Janna was stuck. Part of her felt outrage, built on denial that it was the best solution. There was a core within herself that knew with all their commitments, it was the best they could do.

Danislav was concerned. He hadn't realized the number of people who actively disliked Olaf was so large. "But surely, that can only lead to his death, Lilith. That is *not* the goal here. Those militias represent something of a reaction to the perceived Iron Hand of Boris. Pushing at the edges of his policies. Probing outside the borders of his lands. Chasing bandits that only raided for food and aren't stupid about it, only intimidating the people they take food from."

Danislav frowned at that as he didn't like the policy that allowed raider bands to form. Or the policy that left any bandits on the borders.

The problem was if they went after the pure bandits as well as the sadistic bastards, they'd be stretched well beyond their breaking point. They just didn't have the resources, even with every advantage they had built up. The bandits, rather than the psychopaths, usually protected those they preyed upon from other predators. Boris was somewhat philosophical about it. After all, sometimes Cossacks had practiced similar banditry.

Boris could only protect so much land, so many people. Beyond that, all he could do was encourage restraint as firmly as possible. Prevent the worst atrocities.

That was despite controlling one of the very few areas that still produced ammunition at all. Boris had managed to relocate a small production facility for artillery ammunition as well as ammunition for their rifles. With the efforts to minimize artillery use, they had a decent supply for even a significant period of conflict.

"Your analysis is flawed, Danislav. After the platoons he patrols with most regularly, often filling in for injured or ill privates and NCOs, the self-formed militias are the group most likely to support him. They view him as the 'imprisoned heir.' Although, they won't be easy to lead. They all have their preconceptions of Olaf, and few in the militias have served with him." Boris concluded

Boris was smart enough to allow those militias to form, even let them send officers and senior members to train in tactics and the military skills they needed. That made their issues as well as their support public. It also encouraged units that were on the official register and that supported him unconditionally to train rigorously. To show those viewed as potentially disloyal the cost of an uprising.

"That brings up the second problem," Janna began in a distant tone, "without any of the militias on the board, we have no reserve for the regulars which will be weakened when, or I suppose *if*, the coalition moves in to quieten the central lands."

Danislav's face lit with a wry smile, "Janna, we're talking about the independent militia, not the official militia. The official militia would resent being sent under Olaf. Many of the more experienced members are still in the official militia because of the independent militia. The biggest problem will be maintaining numbers when we send Olaf's militia away."

He rolled his eyes then continued, "They see themselves as a counterbalance to what they view as youthful exuberance. There is only a handful of the pro-Olaf militias. There is barely a half-dozen in each group that are from the first generation after the Fall, and I can only think of one or two who were born before the world's worst day ever."

Boris slowly nodded and, tapping an index finger on his chin, said, "So, they're similar to the gangs that would spontaneously form in large Russian cities?"

Lilith responded, "In analytics of formation, you would be correct. In all other definitions, you would be incorrect. They hold themselves to a much higher standard than any boy gang could, complemented by the compulsory military training that all citizens of your domain must take between the ages of sixteen and twenty, and the year's military service at age twenty-one.

"Their discipline and cohesion I would estimate to be equal to that of a well-drilled militia, perhaps even a reserve force. Similar in nature to the best of the militias in pre-Fall Cold War United States. Call them the Minutemen. I will state unequivocally they do not match the discipline of your regular army, and would have no real threat value in insurrection despite knowledge of your methods of operation.

"In part, this could be due to their estimate of their own abilities compared to your regular forces. Additionally, it would be because of the lack of any tactical heavy weapons or support artillery. Finally, the Weres in their formations are also loyal to Boris as pack leader." Everyone at the table nodded in understanding.

Although the entire population of his domain was expected to be proficient with a rifled sidearm, the official militia was limited to light field artillery. They had a limited number of pieces. Only the regular and reserve forces had medium pieces and infantry mortars. Given the state of the region, most of the military bases had been raided for equipment early on. The independent militias were not allowed any artillery.

Then there was the respect most of Boris' population felt for him.

If rebels lacked a broad support base to move and conceal a stockpile of heavier weapons from a new-found cache, any rebellion would fail and do so quickly. Given that Boris was respected —and at least liked—by most of his citizens, it was doubtful that such an event had even occurred once. Without the occurrence of such an event, no rebellion could succeed, hence the formation of dissidents into independent militias.

They could make it clear that to push too hard against their wishes would cost Boris.

All this made a few additional problems clear to him.

"I'm going to have to slice at least an artillery platoon out of rotation to support whatever forces we end up sending with Olaf. He is going up against an unknown weapon. I won't have him and his forces more vulnerable than necessary. Maybe not any heavier field artillery, but he'll need mortars."

Danislav nodded and said, "I would suggest that some of the original pack would be willing to act as a headquarters squad and bodyguards. If we pick from outside the potential Alphas, there won't be any whispers. Just you doing what you had to for your kids when you sent them away. There might be a little chaos in the sub-packs as people vie for position to be potential replacements. Always will be, though."

A sad smile crossed Danislav's face, and the century or more of life he'd lived seemed to show at once. His voice wavered as he spoke again, "That's the cost of having so many Shifters in your domain. When a position they value comes up, there's always violence." In a weary, resigned move, he briefly scrubbed his face with his hands.

When he looked up, he saw a pair of sorrow-filled parents. He understood part of their concern. For while Olaf could best even his father in bear form, he'd never taken the Pricolici form. They couldn't see that he was as mature as his siblings or themselves without it.

Especially Boris. He was of a different age and felt that his heir should be able to do anything he could. If one of Olaf's siblings could take the Pricolici form, they would have been Boris's heir in a heartbeat.

Sighing, he stood and nodded to the grieving couple. It was a joyous kind of grief, but, finally, their last child was leaving the nest. No parent felt only joy in such a situation, especially when others forced their hands.

He would make sure the send-off was well-oiled, organized, and happened as soon as possible. That was the best he could do.

Boris was too conflicted to give the orders to Olaf. He didn't want to send his eldest son into battle. He didn't want his son to live the life he had. Unfortunately, his son had been born into a time worse than any Boris had lived through before the Fall.

Though there were centers of light, beacons of hope scattered across the world, most of it had descended into violent feudalism of one sort or another.

CHAPTER TWO

Danislav first checked the roster and saw that Olaf should be home. Since he was back, and it was daytime, he'd be training somewhere in the central barracks site. Boris had also insisted on sending a squad from the experienced pack members. He'd attempted to convince Danislav to assist in command, but Janna had reluctantly pointed out that Danislav was too much Boris's right-hand man.

No-one would believe Olaf was in command if Danislav went with him. In the end, Danislav had agreed to find ten or so volunteers from the core pack that went wherever Boris traveled.

At least they understood the motivations Boris had in keeping Olaf back. They'd lived through the Fall. They may not be willing to unconditionally accept Olaf as a competent field commander, but they would protect him to the death on Boris's behalf. They might not have agreed with how he had treated his heir, but they understood the why.

He was entitled to some mistakes after the shit he had pulled them as well as their families out of.

When Danislav finally tracked Olaf down, he was training a mixed group of normals and Shifters in human form. They went through how two or three humans should take on a single Shifter if spotted, just to be safe.

The fact that humans could face Shifters with a reasonable chance of success was one of the factors that allowed for equal status. The fact that every human and Shifter was issued a silver laced blade and a clip of silver ammo for their sidearm was another reason Shifters hadn't tried to push for 'extra' rights now they were common knowledge. Boris's opinion on the matter was the final reason.

Olaf and three of the Shifters were supervising. The standard tactic for unarmed humans against Shifters in human form was for one to tackle at the waist, a second to grapple the arms, and a third to strike from behind. It required some luck, to be sure, and an excess of numbers.

They taught the larger men and the largest women tactics for taking on Shifters one on one. Unfortunately, not everyone was up to the Queen Bitch's Guard standards. That meant they had to find tactics that worked for less than the perfect warrior physique.

Boris was still the leader of the Siberian Shifter community, officially. He needed to be the one that judged if a Shifter was breaking his code. In these days, the Strictures were impossible to enforce.

All the Shifters in Siberia were welcome to move to his domain if they chose, as long as they were willing to follow the laws of the land. Many simply loved living on the open steppe despite the swampy mess that the tundra had become. So, they had to follow Boris's code.

Boris's code was not hard to follow. Harm not those weaker than yourself. Seek to protect. If you must steal, no more than your needs for a week and a day. It was the best he could do when he traveled across the steppes for a month a year.

Once a year, most years at least, Boris and the central pack traveled to mete justice to his Siberian pack. First offenses were held over until he arrived. Repeat offenders might be brought into New Romanovka or punished in place by neighboring Shifters. Occasionally, a troublemaking individual or small group would make it to his borders. Capturing them when they did was a point of pride.

Boris hated wasting potential, but at least one in three of the captures was too feral for life in his pack. They were too unwilling to change their ways for a second chance. And it was slowly getting worse.

Still, it was a problem for another day.

Danislav started out of his contemplation when Olaf shouted happily, "Older brother, so good to see you! Join me on the mats?"

Danislav smiled and nodded. The room went silent. In human form, Boris and Danislav were slightly better than Olaf. They had years more experience, but they couldn't give him any slack. It was bittersweet for Danislav. Strangely, Olaf had become the brother in truth that he wasn't in blood. Returning home from a patrol with Olaf gone would be like part of the foundations of his life being stripped away.

But his brother needed the experience. He needed to spread his wings, whatever the risk. Danislav's thoughts were racing, distracting him as he blocked a series of light punches and kicks. Probing blows, seeing where his head was at.

A sound kick to the guts brought him back fully to the sparring room. Olaf looked at Danislav quizzically. Such a basic series of attacks shouldn't have gotten through. Shaking himself as he backed up and repositioned, Danislav focused. He couldn't have Olaf think that he'd let him win.

Sparring back and forth between the two was going fast enough that the training in the rest of the gym had stopped as they watched a pair of masters. Strikes flowed back and forth as if they were in some intricately choreographed dance. Only the force of the blows, the sharp thwacks and whacks as hits were blocked or redirected, told the audience that this was serious training. To many of the watchers, it was training at an intensity they had never achieved.

Olaf threw a palm strike to the head, following it with a rising elbow and a feinting kick to Danislav's knee. Despite blocking the elbow and sidestepping the kick, Danislav hadn't expected Olaf to pivot on his back foot and rip his feinting foot forward, knocking Danislav onto his back.

Chagrin filled Danislav as he found himself grabbed by the foot and dragged forward. Danislav managed to kick his hand and grabbed him, but only realized that Olaf had let go to shove him in the back and grab his arms as he tried to roll away. The younger brother had improved significantly since they had last sparred about a year ago.

It was odd how training people who did not know martial arts could improve you as fast in some ways as training with people near your skill level. Every time you taught someone, you learned something yourself.

After all, wasn't there an old saying that the world's best swordsman didn't fear the second best? He feared the worst because he couldn't predict what the damned fool would do.

"Mercy," Danislav grunted out, admitting defeat. As he rolled on his back and caught his breath, rubbing his wrists from the tight hold Olaf had captured them in, he saw a genuine smile on his brother's face. "You've gotten better," he complimented the young man.

He did take after his mother. Six-foot-three, but more wiry than bulky. Still, Olaf was stronger than any Werewolf. He was also the fastest Were in animal form that anyone Danislav talked to had ever encountered. Even with Danislav leading a team to train Olaf, they'd stopped sparring in animal form ten years ago. He regularly beat his father in bear form. That should have been enough to earn him a spot leading outer patrols.

'Damn his parents' overprotectiveness,' Danislav thought.

All of Olaf's siblings had been given tasks years ago. Fiona was helping the Mongolian pack against the Sacred Clans. His youngest brothers, the twins Anatoly and Leo, had been scouting the central regions and acting as diplomats to the Finnish government—one of the few true governments to survive the Fall. They'd also led missions to contact the rulers of the regions that encompassed the former states of Estonia, Latvia, and the reinvigorated royalty of Sweden.

"Why were you so distracted at the start of the fight, brother?" Olaf asked, confusion on his face. "I know you, and you know I'm skilled. You wouldn't let something as basic as that go through unless you had something on your mind. Tell me," he finished, an almost childish anticipation in his expression. The hope was clear on Olaf's face that he might be given the news he had been prodding his brother for over the last twenty years.

"Yes, brother, it is. Circumstances have finally conspired to force Father to give you command."

It was apparent that Olaf wanted to react childishly. Backflips, perhaps, or maybe a simple shout of joy, but he kept it contained.

He had been denied the opportunity to prove himself for so long, he'd been convinced it would never come. To be fair, few people would have blamed him. Those who distrusted his competence would be thrilled about Boris sending Olaf on what, to them, would seem like a secondary priority. Especially considering the forces he would be sent with.

Those who were more disappointed in Boris for giving Olaf no opportunity to prove himself would be happy that he was finally given a chance.

Reaching down and grabbing his brother's wrist, Olaf hauled him to his feet. "Come, brother," his voice boomed through the room expansively, "we have much to plan if we are to get things moving quickly. And the sooner we get things moving, the less chance there is of my father changing his mind."

With that, he turned towards the door. After dusting himself off, Danislav followed him, a smile on his face. Olaf was usually so reserved, hiding everything behind the mask and burying his frustration deep. Maybe this was what he needed to move forward. Perhaps this was his chance to become someone with open emotions that others could respect, rather than a distant man they felt held them in disdain.

CHAPTER THREE

Olaf and Danislav found themselves going over the table, looking at the organization for the proposed force to send south-west towards what had once been the Ukraine and Belarus. Even fifty years of winters with minimal repairs hadn't destroyed the highways. Without heavy trucks constantly running along them and breaking them down, the lighter traffic preserved them for the most part, and they were still more than adequate.

That was key to Boris's military planning. With those roads mostly intact, his special logistics support concepts came to the fore. In winter, it was dogs and sleds. Now in mid-spring, the concrete and asphalt highways played a major role in his success, as did his bicycle design.

With the breakdown of most of the oil industry, cars, trucks, and armored vehicles had to be used sparingly. New ones couldn't be built anyway, with what limited heavy industry was available. The few heavy tanks they had managed to scavenge shortly after the Fall were mostly in bunkers around Lilith's caves —that site was too important to risk falling into anyone else's hands.

His history as a Cossack had taught Boris an important lesson about horses. Even though his artillery still used them, they ate a lot every day. That made them a logistical nightmare. The fact that they were better off-road than even wide-rimmed bicycles made up for that liability with artillery. But his infantry was trained as a form of 'Dragoon,' mounted infantry.

The major difference was that the 'mount' was a specially designed pedal-powered bike. It was something that had repeatedly been used from the middle of the twentieth century AD.

Boris's single logistics battalion was fitted entirely on tricycles with a wagon bed on the back. These vehicles could carry well in excess of a ton of supplies each with trained riders. Normal bikes were restricted, even with modifications and a trailer, to three-quarters of a ton.

Overall, the logistical capability was a trick stolen from the Vietnamese in their wars of the 1960s and 1970s. Without helicopters to interdict the supplies, or aircraft to bomb the roads, Boris was immensely confident his logistics would be nearly impossible to cut. If someone managed to get a force across his supply lines, then his Were patrols would savage it.

Not to mention every soldier in his forces was trained as a rifleman first.

Olaf planned to scavenge a platoon for rear base security from the two companies being sent to the town. He would need to base troops forward if it was a Vampire trying to be clever. The Vampire could have tested the weapon hundreds of kilometers away from its base to hide where that was located. Time and distance meant little to Forsaken Vampires.

As they would be under orders to have flanking patrols, that made sense from a logistical point of view for his force and security for the main position. Basing his logistics forward was a risk. The risk was counterbalanced by many advantages if this had been a raid to ensure a buffer zone by whatever opposition was out there. That seemed most likely, considering all the supplies they had left untouched in the cellars. Especially since they had left no guards.

"We'll call up the *Amazon* militia first," Olaf stated to Danislav.

Being of the old school, Danislav's jaw hit the floor. He felt that women in the infantry were a liability. They couldn't cope as well, and some of their equipment was a manifestly different shape to accommodate a differing body form. Their packs, in particular, sat on the hip rather than the shoulder.

"Danislav, I have to prove myself to the people as a leader. Father never worries about having women in integrated positions serving. Only a few of the *old hands*," he paused to grin at his foster brother, "have any issue with it. The main difference is the *Amazons* train harder than any other militia to prove themselves capable. I need that self-confidence in their ability."

The *Amazons* had formed to prove a purely female force could be as capable as any male or mixed force. They held themselves to a high standard in training, and their commander, Major Petrova, was desperate to get them deployed. She reported them as ready, but there seemed to be some equivocation on their ability to co-operate with other units. That was what made Danislav most nervous, especially with Olaf having only a battalion to run a Search and Destroy mission.

Slowly, grudgingly, Danislav nodded. "And they aren't listed on our force lists. That gives you a so-called company that you can use to strengthen your numbers." The *Amazons* trained as fourteen-person squads, and only had any training with light mortars. Not the medium mortars the integrated units also had occasional practice on.

"Also, and this is more from a strategic perspective, they will be perceived by any local townspeople as less of a threat. They will give us a better way to communicate with the locals because of this. Finally, if they have overestimated their ability in the field, I can still use them for positional defense."

Danislav grunted. That was true. Every adult in Boris's region was capable with gun or bow from a defensive position. Even many of the teenagers were. Hunting was a major supplement of foodstuffs. The extra meat for normal humans over the still bitter winters helped survival in the smaller villages and farmsteads. For Weres, it became a competition with the normals.

Since many of the independent settlements surrounding Boris had no ammunition, even if they had guns, bows had made a comeback. Just about every person in the militias could make an arrow, even if the accuracy of their product was inferior. Some weapon was better than no weapon.

In some ways, Olaf felt that it was better this way—being in command of regular forces, he would have been continuously second-guessed. Leading militia forces, they at least had some respect for his abilities. Their officers had some respect for him. He had pushed his father to treat them as auxiliaries and to call them up for training on special weapons.

Boris had insisted on keeping the heavier weapons only in the central armories, but that was reasonable. He was, after all, the ruler and had seen how different people could react poorly to harsh situations. By controlling the heavier weapons and ruling with a light hand, he had the respect of most of his people. Those who didn't respect his rule could see the price of rebelling against it. They learned to fear the possible consequences. Especially when he took no action against those who left his lands quietly.

Unless, of course, they took up banditry. Boris considered that rebellion if they had been from his lands. He responded firmly and violently to it. There were no survivors from bandits who had originated from his lands.

By the end of the day, in addition to the *Amazons*, Olaf had chosen a company from the eastern, western, and the southern lands. All the militias in the north were already tasked to either head west or to patrol against Finnish treachery. Allies were only to be trusted so far in Boris's opinion. He'd seen betrayal too often.

It annoyed Olaf, as one of the better Were packs was a northern militia. They were the most annoyed with the restrictions on Olaf's deployment with the reserve company. But hopefully with the pick of the newest recruit training, he'd have a heavy battalion.

As it was, he'd have to re-organize the militia units he had coming to make the best use of the Weres. He'd only have two pure platoons of them, considering the disproportionate number of Weres who were NCOs or Officers, especially in the militias. He would be able to pull a dozen from the *Amazons*. The rest would be needed to be machine gunners, or carry and operate other heavy weapons.

"Brother, are you sure about your choices?" Danislav asked once they'd gone over the plan. "You're gonna have to spend at least a month re-training them with the unit changes."

Olaf only shrugged.

"It's not like I have that much choice, Danny," Olaf said. Danislav scowled at the use of the nickname, then shook himself. Olaf continued, "Half the militias are formed of older men and women. Useful for defense only. That single good southern militia *isn't* that great at patrolling or stealth. They train almost exclusively for assaults. With the *Amazons*, who aren't listed on your original list, I'll have a battalion reinforced with an oversized company. If I manage to poach some of the recruits that should finish training around then, I can push that up to nearly two companies. Most of our mission will be search and engage patrolling, but it doesn't seem likely that the Ukraine/Belarus region will have much of a force left. The entire region came apart during the Fall."

Danislav grunted his agreement. They'd gotten a few refugees from the Ukraine/Belarus region over the years, and it was a disaster area. Every faction had taken up arms, and the country had been a war zone for at least thirty years. Although Boris hadn't investigated it for the last ten years, it had only recently been recovering to small organized towns. Usually under one strongman or another. Most of the towns of a decade ago would have struggled to muster a platoon of men with the ability and inclination to soldier.

"Keep it to platoon strength, minimum. You need the show of force," Danislav said.

Olaf had other ideas—and other plans. Squads patrolling, with platoons to support upon contact. Now was not the time to tell his brother. He might get worried enough to tell their father.

Still, it was a shoestring operation. Olaf was going to have to act as the rapier to the other side's hammer. Clear operational room, find out what they had, if possible capture samples, then return. Any intelligence they captured or gathered along the way would be a bonus.

Any group that wiped out a village to test something had a brainless leader, or the leader relied on fear. The biggest bonus they could find would be if the leader of the region had rats in his woodwork. At least Olaf had a fallback location.

There were the two companies that had been sent to fortify and man the town Danislav had found. It was now being called 'Hope Rebuilt' by the locals from the farmsteads surrounding it.

CHAPTER FOUR

"Father, if you let me take one of the shuttles then it will under-mine the troops' perceptions of me as a leader!" Olaf shouted. The shuttles hadn't been used much for fear of attracting more attention than they already did. They were one of the few eastern European regions that produced regular surpluses.

"Nonsense. I'll be using one as my headquarters, and I'll have three available for troop movement. Unlike you, I don't need any, but they will reduce casualties, and things have calmed enough that using them makes good sense. Everyone is rebuilding from the Fall. Showing that we have some of the highest tech available before the Fall can only protect us all, for now," Boris shouted back at his son.

The new manufacturing capacity would be coming online in the cave soon, and soon after, the Arkhangelsk works would go live. It would take time, but progress was being made.

More quietly, Boris continued, "We have those manufacturing plants going live. With their ability to produce 'Kurtherian' tech, we need to show we can defend them from the start. Otherwise, we are a big, fat target for someone."

Olaf continued to glare at his father, then responded through gritted teeth. "Isn't that convenient? So, you are claiming the fact that locking me in that flying coffin won't protect me better than anything else you could provide?"

"Who said anything about locking you in it?" Boris answered angrily. He knew that no Were would put up with that. Part of the reason he was sending his son was the hope that he would find a way to change to a third form.

Olaf only snorted and said, "If it's the C&C center, then I'll have to be there if we face a major battle."

Boris raised an eyebrow, then answered in a deceptive calm, "That was a consideration." When Olaf went to interject, Boris raised a hand and continued "But it was far from the largest one. The largest one was far simpler—we know the other side you could run into has Alien weaponry. Either that, or some form of Earth weapon I've never heard of. Whomever I would send to lead the southern force would be taking a shuttle to counter that. If you keep arguing with me, I will send someone else. And the shuttle."

"Besides, if such weaponry is used, you'll be in the greatest danger." Boris continued, pain in his voice. "You'll have a backup command post, but if there is a weapon that can damage the shuttle, you'll face the most danger."

Olaf opened his mouth, then shut it. The stormy expression on his father's face told him the line had been drawn. He also hadn't said the shuttle could only be used for command and control purposes.

It had a capable sensor suite and had modifications to enable both etheric and radio transmissions.

Beyond that, he could use it to make several trips with extra equipment for the forward base, and scout the areas around the new headquarters being established in the town that had been emptied.

Yes. He could make this work. First, he needed to prevent his father from realizing his plans. Hardening the mulish expression on his face, he turned on his heel and stormed from the room. He heard Boris mutter, "I wish he hadn't inherited his mother's temper."

A smile quirked his face as he thought '*if only you knew I had some of her talents for deception as well, Father.*' He continued stomping down the hallway so as not to let his father in on that little secret.

Two thoughts remained floating in his head. First, *what father doesn't know can't hurt him.* Secondly, *actions taken without orders were not actions taken against orders.*

CHAPTER FIVE

Olaf was troubled. The check training had gone as well as could be expected. The *Amazons* were an outstanding unit overall when it came to the exercises that checked their training. However, they brought other problems. They were xenophobic towards working with male units and accepting advice from male trainers. They also were weak in an assault and refused to accept the fact that they were outmatched at that task by the western and southern companies in those exercises.

He was going to have to get creative. He needed to break that xenophobia. If necessary, replacements for their unit might have to come from the other militia units. They had a four in five chance of being male. The *Amazons* needed to be able to have any empty slots filled, or he couldn't take them.

In any military organization, only so much divergence could be allowed. The outright hostility to men had to go, or Olaf would be forced to take action. In this case, it would be the formal disbandment of the unit. It would prove dangerous and possibly even toxic to any mixed or all-male unit it served beside with its current base.

He decided to pit the units against each other in shield wall or phalanx formations without the spears. The last thing he needed was live weapons against each other. While the *Amazons* were capable, they lacked the sheer mass that was an advantage in phalanx and shield wall combat. Nor were they willing to take advice on technique from people in other units. It would also be useful as a physical conditioning and team building exercise.

Before she had left, Gyada convinced Boris the value of such training. The regulars competed as squads and platoons using it. It had almost become a sport amongst them. One the militias rarely practiced.

The weighted shields were just sitting there. It was time to put them to use.

Predictably, the lower ranks in all the militia units complained. They didn't see the broader point of the training. The things it could teach them as a unit that no other training would.

That they could depend on the man to their left or their right. That they were stronger acting as a unit than individuals.

After the *Amazons* had been trounced for several hours, he offered to even up the matchup. He would put individual *Amazons* into slots in the other unit's squads currently held down by women. They jumped at the chance to prove themselves.

Then, he put them against other squads from the same southern militia in which he had not allowed substitutions. The results were interesting.

They mostly held back, uncertain about the others around them. In a couple of cases, the reverse was true. They pushed forward too hard and too fast, creating a gap that doomed the phalanx formation. This displayed a lack of teamwork that a military unit relied on, especially for assaults. Everyone depended on those around them to do their job, and do it right, or it could go to hell in a handbasket even without any casualties before contact.

With the inevitable casualties in such an action, without the trust in a unit, the assault would almost inevitably fail. It wasn't that the *Amazons* had no trust. It was that there had been a deficiency in their training in building the trust to the level necessary in a soldier.

By the end of the first day, they were learning. Much more slowly, they were also developing a sense of comradery with the other units. However, watching the interactions, one of the regular officers reviewing performance thought he saw the problems.

The first problem was, although a capable combat leader, Major Valerie Petrova, wasn't paying attention to her officers' actions out of training exercises and assessments. The more common problem was that there was a promoted officer micromanaging things. Her issue was a disregard for the necessary management of officers and noncoms.

All officers and senior noncoms, even in the self-forming militia, were required to be trained and assessed. Unfortunately, continuing assessment was weak in the militia in general. Practically non-existent for the independent militias. Petrova would be reprimanded.

The assessing officer, Captain Erisov, liked a challenge. Sergeant Ivonika and Lieutenant Nimenen were shaping the unit to their prejudices. Both had been abused by men at some point in their life.

For Ivonika, it was a private, family issue. Those involved had been executed by Boris. Nimenen had been rescued from a group of particularly vicious bandits, as had her mother. Her dislike of men could be a dangerous thing.

For all that, they were both good soldiers, fully trained. Captain Erisov thought they could be salvaged, but agreed with Olaf that they were a substantial factor in making the *Amazons* undeployable. Their strong personalities and opinions were not being countered or channeled by the officers above them.

On the other hand, for a combat deployment, Major Petrova

was a viable choice. After the deployment, she'd need to be either re-trained or replaced.

She was tactically and strategically sound. She was decisive without undermining her subordinates. Unfortunately, her lack of interest in the administration of the unit had resulted in these problems. But because of her competence in action, her shortcomings had avoided undermining her authority.

It still needed to be dealt with. And while substituting a shiny new lieutenant and a sergeant being called back from retirement were not the best options, they were the only ones available.

In fact, one of the militia units had been operating with only one lieutenant, despite having a full complement of higher officers. Another had been keeping several sergeants on the books, despite none of these men being field capable. Several units were operating short squads.

In bringing the squads up to strength, the *Amazons* were vital. Their oversized squads allowed Olaf to find those who had been willing to work with other units by the end of training and transfer some experienced personnel across to the shorthanded units. As a result, they dragged in most of the female recruits to maintain their designated squad size. This kept the *Amazons* at their authorized strength while avoiding the problems of too many rookies in his other units.

For the other problems, he was mostly forced to put in shiny new sergeants and lieutenants. He even transferred a few of his assigned bodyguards into sergeant slots, swapping them for reliable men from the units they were moved to. This helped build *esprit de corps* for the new battalion. He was trusting picked men from each of their units to be by his side if the shit hit the fan.

In addition to drill, training and assessment exercises, and individual task training, the officers were trained in tactics and strategy while using old style sandboard exercises.

It took a total of five weeks to get the unit gathered, re-trained, and ready for movement. At least they had all been re-equipped with the regular's standard issue rifles, AK-74Ms that had been plentiful in one of the supply dumps that had been captured years ago.

All the militias usually had was the AK-74. The ubiquitous AK-47 had not been used by Boris's forces. The AK-74 was superior, as was the more expensive, modified AK-74M. Both were within his limited production capabilities. Each troop also had a Makarov pistol. The final issue weapon in his forces was a hammer-backed Tomahawk that doubled as a tool in the field.

Most of the materials for weapons were being reclaimed from abandoned vehicles and scrap metal, although limited trade with Finland provided an additional source of minerals for the brass in the rounds they preferred.

Light body armor made of a material that one of the modified crops that Lilith created for them was used instead of the synthetic body armor that was ubiquitous in the early twenty-first century. Incorporating metals and silica into its fibers as it grew, it had superior stopping power to the ceramic plates in many early twenty-first century armors, and lighter weight. It also grew the fibers long and ready for weaving. The biggest problem with it was that special tools were needed to cut it.

The specialty weapons were also manufacturable in the facilities Boris had up and running. Slightly less accurate than western sub guns, the BIZON was still a preferred weapon for a scout due to its standard-issue flash suppressor and silencer.

The marksmen and snipers were equipped with Dragunov rifles. Because of ammunition compatibility considerations, Boris had chosen the RPK-74M as the squad light machine gun. Several AA-12 fully automatic shotguns for close combat assaults were distributed amongst every squad as they saw fit.

At the end of the on-base training, they had a movement to complete. Olaf had arranged with Boris to have some surprise exercises en-route to their interim destination, the new base being set up in the ruins of the town that Danislav had found.

The training incorporated into their early movement was to operate against an enemy unit inside their territory. It could involve anything from being ambushed to an all out assault on an enemy position.

Training rounds had been issued, and during the first days of the movement, they were all that was allowed to be in magazines loaded into the weapons. Live magazines were issued, but not loaded into their rifles.

The training rounds were a pain, but Lilith had come up with a compound that was dense enough to be fired like a standard bullet and acted as a marker on a hit. The marker rounds left residue in any gun barrel, and cleaning was an issue. They were better than previous attempts with training rounds, but would affect the accuracy of subsequent shots fired through the barrel before cleaning.

They also taught a lesson by leaving significant bruises on areas hit outside the body armor.

Going to live ammunition was only permitted after 'Red Wolf' went over the radio. The exercise answer and response challenge was to be 'Lair' and 'Hunter One.'

Still, within the week they would be on the final leg of their journey, to their proposed base camp. Then Olaf would call in the shuttle, and their real mission would start.

CHAPTER SIX

Olaf was cursing his father. Boris had sent in two companies of regulars and a company of militia as his opposition force. They had been sent to ambush and block the route. From the appearance of the dug in and camouflaged bunkers in front of him, three on each side of the road, they'd been sent in early, as well.

He assumed it had been at least ten days ago to get the positions so well camouflaged that the scouting squad had been wiped out before they had a clue there was an enemy force there. They could be seen on the ground playing dead as the main body approached. The opposition force soldiers that had moved up from the bunkers to remove the 'bodies' scurried back at the approach of Olaf's force.

While it was unfortunate that the scouts had been killed for the exercise, they had done part of their job. To prevent a devastating ambush or spot it. The gunfire had prevented an overwhelming assault. The bruises would remind the scouts to be more cautious and observant.

There were the concerns amongst the officer trained members of his bodyguards about the attitudes towards men that were lingering in close to a quarter of the *Amazons*.

There were reasons that Olaf was comfortable with the exercise, despite the past influence on the *Amazon's* rogue lieutenant and sergeant. First, even with the occasional continuing incident, they were overcoming their dislike of men.

They were seeing that not all male soldiers were like those that their former leaders had told them to fear. That they were people. Good, bad, and indifferent, just like women. This had been helped by mixing some of those with reservations—but not outright hostility—with the other units. They were willing to work with the men in their new units, and none of the men in those formations treated them with any disrespect.

Beyond that, there was the fear of the consequences. The punishment for a soldier harming another soldier outside the parameters of training was draconian and could possibly kill the perpetrator. Depending on the situation, it could be from ten years of hard labor or worse. Killing a fellow soldier with live ammunition would be a life sentence as a servant to the soldier's kin, with them having the power of life or death over the perpetrator.

Finally, now that the problem had been rubbed in her face, Major Petrova was acting with energy and dispatch to stamp out any active action concerning what she referred to as 'personal opinions.' She had randomly inspected the ammunition loaded into twenty-eight weapons on the first morning of the march. When one was found with live ammunition, she had called in officers from other units to have every gun inspected.

Two more were found with live ammunition. Those three soldiers were stripped of gear and sent under the guard of the base police for charges to be laid. A court-martial was ordered. Their squadmates were given extra duty and an additional watch for three days on the march as punishment for failure to report the infraction. The two lieutenants in command of the platoons those squads were in also received punishment.

Those who still held a dislike of men, for whatever reason,

were being very quiet about it. Major Petrova's mother had been raped and beaten to within an inch of her life in the early years after the Fall of society. She knew what caused the hatred.

She would not brook it, endangering the force that saved her from the same fate—that had taken her mother and herself in. Olaf suspected there would be some quiet conversations with the women who held to that hatred over the march.

But that still left Olaf with the problem of how to take the bunkers without using the artillery platoon. The grass was always relatively short at this time of year, so sneaking up in the day would be impossible. Even at night, it would be difficult. All it would take to expose a unit attempting such an action was one man with thermal equipment.

He scowled at the map, then noticed a crossroads with a dirt track several kilometers back. Turning to his subordinate officers, he pointed to it. "This is our best chance. We use the track to get two companies behind them using the bikes as far as we can. We strip the units down to two days rations and ammunition. If we strip the Shifters out of their squads, we'll have a platoon of scouts—a squad forward and one to sweep each flank. The rest of their unit can split their equipment loads.

"Two of the other companies to dig in fighting positions just outside of rifle range, and the final company would make closer flanking movements on the same side as our unit will be circling. Distract them."

Slowly, Major Petrova and the four senior captains nodded their heads.

"Sir, I request that the *Amazons* be one of the units picked for the main flanking maneuver. They need more practice at assaulting fortifications."

Olaf frowned, but regretfully shook his head. "No. We are going up against regulars. Besides, if they are one of the units digging into fighting positions, they will have the opportunity to assault once the surprise attack goes in. If we do poorly enough here, Boris may pull everyone off this operation. None of us want that after the last month. We need to work as a unit, and for that, we need the best two assault units in the flanking movement.

"Besides, you are the second-ranking officer. I need you here to command this half of the assault. I also need you here to assault those fortifications if they decide that my flanking maneuver is the main force. If they come after us in strength and weaken those bunkers by a company or more, you are to assault them as soon as the departing force is clear. You'll need to keep in contact with Ivanov's company to do that." Ivanov's eastern militia was better at feint maneuvers than the other unit he was planning on leaving with Petrova. "And make sure you have a platoon covering each company's rear."

Sighing, the Major nodded in agreement. At least her girls wouldn't be in the distraction force. Just in the lower risk offensive. If nothing else, it would help them build confidence. That was as important to a unit in some ways as actual skill. A unit with no confidence would never be able to carry through in a real action anyway.

After organizing the movement and planning for the covering units to be ready to attack from two a.m., Olaf and his bodyguards joined the flanking maneuver.

With wolves on the flank, he pushed the units hard. The quicker they moved close to the position behind the enemy force, the better. There was howling on his left flank in the distance and gunfire. Probably enemy scouts engaging his distraction. He only hoped that there wasn't an enemy unit patrolling this flank in force. There was only room for two companies to be dug in in the entrenchments.

Olaf became lost in thought. That meant at least one company was outside the fortifications. Worse, rather than trench or open fortifications, they had covered bunkers. Even if Olaf had training rounds for his artillery, none of his artillery was strong enough to damage the bunkers or their interlocking fire zones.

Besides, even though Boris had some facility to produce shells, he didn't waste any of it on training rounds for interunit exercises.

His artillery trained for hip shooting at a target. They never fired in training at friendly units. For the training exercises that simulated artillery attack, pre-positioned charges were dug in. They even simulated artillery effects from guns larger than any Boris used in the field. He did have a dozen camouflaged heavy cannons around both Arkhangelsk and New Romonovka. The railguns still covered the cave itself, but there was now only a fifty-meter kill zone around them.

Shaking his head, Olaf brought himself back to the present. They had about five hours to cycle around thirty-five kilometers to travel wide enough of the fortifications to make the plan viable. They had to circle so wide of the fortifications to reduce the chance of any patrols spotting them.

It was a gamble, like everything in war. Given the training mission parameters, there were as good odds as he could engineer. The other option was to use Weres as other forces Arkhangelsk Palden had encountered. Since the Fall, there were two variations that had been encountered by Boris's force. Shock troops or leader's bodyguard.

Neither took full advantage of a Were's abilities. Both stemmed from a belief that they were more valuable than their human compatriots. Boris had lived a long time. He had concluded that Weres were merely different. Perhaps they were more powerful in some ways, but that didn't make them more valuable.

It caused those who led troops with a group of known Weres to use them in a way that was less than optimal for the force as a whole. Boris's units were fully integrated and tried to have at least one Were in each squad. Most often they would be the designated scout, although in teams that specialized in assaulting building or fortifications, they were usually given machine guns for entry instead.

The simple fact was there had always been fewer Weres than humans. They could be used to improve the survival rates of a force as a whole, or they could be used as a last resort. Boris had shown in several actions against various warlords that the latter was a losing hand against the former.

Still, people followed the same pattern as it worked well against everyone except Boris.

<<<>>>

It was cool in the evening, and a dry chill had settled in the air as Olaf prepared his companies for a nighttime assault. Four platoons were assigned a bunker each to assault, with the other four platoons to lay down covering fire.

They were crawling through the grass and once they were within a hundred meters, the second group would stop moving and start firing at the bunker slits. They were offset from their comrade's line of advance to reduce friendly fire risk.

They were not spotted. The clicks came over the radio, indicating the two platoons were in position. Boris flicked his radio to all frequencies and transmitted "Lair" over the open channels.

A surprised, "Hunter One," transmitted across the radio. As it did, the two assigned platoons were primed. They waited another ten minutes—as long as they thought they could risk. Then they started firing to distract the bunkers from the troops moving up on them.

Return fire from the bunkers facing his force was somewhat sporadic at first. It steadily increased as more rifles turned to face the firing platoons. That would also kill the firers' night vision, improving the chances of those still sneaking forward in some ways.

While they didn't have training frag grenades, they did have smoke grenades. For exercise purposes, if a smoke grenade was successfully thrown into a bunker, it would be considered out of action, and the troops manning it were casualties. That removed concussive risk to the occupants as well.

To his surprise, he heard artillery fire from the east. Rather than the explosion he had almost feared when he heard them, he saw the blaze and billow of smoke rounds. He was ashamed not to have thought of them. Major Petrova would be a significant asset to his force, despite any failings, it was obvious.

Soon, two of the bunkers his force had been targeting were billowing smoke. The platoons that had been targeting them shifted around to the remaining bunkers on their fronts. As they rose, a hidden bunker that had not been spotted by the scouts or himself took them under fire. As they started falling, a platoon or more started boiling out of a completely underground dugout.

With his two companies pinned down and taking casualties, he had only one force he could throw at the suddenly appearing troops. His companies were already shocked by the sudden fire from an unidentified bunker. If a mobile force hit them, they could break.

Even if they didn't, they would start falling back.

Looking around to his bodyguards and command squad, Olaf shouted, "Follow me!"

He charged into the mess, and a few of his men went down as they charged across the four hundred meters. Still, with the forces already in play and the enemy's loss of two bunkers that were meant to be covering the area he was charging across, it was a reasonably safe tactic. Add to that the sheer surprise of the charge, and Olaf only lost two or three of his command and bodyguard group to incoming fire.

The platoon that had boiled out of the dugout was whipsawed between threats. Once they were within a hundred and fifty meters, the command platoon took a prone position and fired into the standing unit. Looking around, Olaf saw smoke coming out from some of the other bunkers. His troops were moving from target to target.

His part in the combat was over. If he was honest, it was all a little sour in his mouth. Once he set a plan and it went into motion, his part in an operation would often be over.

There was no excitement to be found at his rank unless things went wrong.

<<<>>>

"So, how did my son's force rank in your post-battle analysis, Paul, Lilith?" Over the years, despite or perhaps because of his change into a Were, Paul had slowly withdrawn from the combat forces. He had spent nearly as large a percentage of his life as Boris soldiering. More of it in proportion actively fighting. After the destruction of the world he had known, he'd lost his sense of humor, as well. Eventually, he had become an analyst.

There was also the incident that had so upset Alecta, his wife, that Boris had felt compelled to pull him from the field.

They had fallen out some about twenty years ago when Boris refused to send Olaf on missions with any real danger. Things had been cordial but cool between them. It had taken a large serving of crow, but Boris was making an effort to reach out to Paul now.

For the last twenty-five years, Paul had been responsible for arranging the critique of every operation and training exercise. He also made good use of his schooling in psychology, helping troopers deal with the effects of battle fatigue and combat stress.

Boris longed to see the jester again, the laughing warrior he had known, but events had changed most people. He only had to look at how he had coddled his son. He shied away from the thought.

Paul answered firmly, "Top score this year. Ninety percent. By taking the risk of using an existing and probably known roadway to circle behind the enemy force, he was able to assault a day earlier than most manage. The regulars played the wrong odds on this one. They sent their extra company to screen and ambush along the other side."

"His second in command organized a highly successful assault from her side after his started. By the time the third op-force company arrived, he had two companies manning the fortifications and two patrolling to trap the third company. No criticism of the third op-force company surrendering when they found 'friendly' fortifications occupied by enemies and another force approaching their rear. It was the smart option."

"The only things I find fault with is the casualty rate. Twelve percent killed or wounded is on the high side, even if the ratio was weighted more heavily towards wounded than usual. Also, he should be reprimanded for throwing his command group into the fray as early as he did. It helped... this time. Most of the time, retaining the command group as both a reserve and to improve control of engaged forces is a greater advantage."

Boris sighed and said, "So, he's deployable?"

Paul laid a hand on his friend's shoulder and said, "It would be better if he were deploying as a captain or even a major. Someone who can get it stuck in. But yes, he is deployable as a lieutenant colonel. He claims he only went in with his command group due to no other unit being in position. From where they were positioned before, the fortifications reserve boiled out of the hidden bunker, it is plausible. He has been reprimanded, but he chafes at watching combat without taking part in it."

Boris sighed and turned his face from his friend, saying, "All Weres do, old friend."

Paul put a hand on Boris's shoulder and said softly, "Boris, it is well past time he was sent into the fire. That's the only way to find the mettle of the man you raised. We both know that. You didn't raise a scientist or a farmer. You raised a soldier."

Paul paused and took a deep breath, "He's more likely to survive than most who go into combat, thanks to his heritage. Just trust he will come home."

Boris nodded, but Paul could still see the fear in his body language.

"We all carry some scars, us who lived through the Great Fall," Boris answered softly.

Sighing, Boris flicked his thoughts away with an odd hand movement. "I must go. The representatives will be here soon." Paul nodded. Viktor was from all reports a psychopath. He had inherited command of the realm his father, a successful warlord, had carved out after the disaster.

Viktor's realm was faring poorly after they had been taken over by the psychopath. To maintain it, he'd resorted to raiding. That was causing issues for others with more stable realms. Boris, having the resources to attempt an assault on fortifications without horrendous casualties, had been asked to help by the Finnish Confederation Council.

St Petersburg was a mix of ruined buildings, half-repaired occupied sections, and newly built docks. It would be difficult to take no matter the force. Boris needed to get his game face on for the negotiations.

CHAPTER SEVEN

Boris slammed his fist on the conference table. "No! I will not agree with your plan. You want my forces to take the brunt of the fighting and for Finland, Sweden, and Estonia to divide all the spoils," he roared. "Go find another ally. I know that I can secure my borders—if needs be, against all your forces *combined*! I am willing to help, not get screwed."

There was silence in the room at his explosion. To be fair to Boris, they were asking for him to supply three regiments and his artillery, while the Swedes blockaded the St. Petersburg dock. In exchange, they would provide a regiment each and 'Administer the realm.' Boris had the strong feeling that would mean 'squeeze the realm for our own advantage.'

The Swedes were happy to have their dominion over the Baltic Sea confirmed if they blockaded the port to prevent Viktor escaping. From the edge of a three-mile fishing zone, all shipping would be under their protection and tolls.

All that had been offered to Boris for his commitments was some land he didn't want or need and a minor concession on trading for copper and zinc. While brass case ammunition was nice, he could use steel cases. In fact, a significant portion of his captured stockpiles was steel cased ammo in vacuum packs.

"I suggest you come up with a better deal for my people, who will be paying in blood, than a swathe of land that has little value after what Viktor has done."

There was silence all around. The Estonian was fuming, but the Finn, a Major Nyland, was nodding in agreement. When he spoke up, he said, "And your proposal is?"

"Mutual administration of the entire area, *including St. Petersburg*, until they can form their own neutral state between us all. I will even offer to provide cadre to train a force to protect its southern border for us, recruited from the local populace. While Sweden would not be involved with the overall administration of the region, they should have a say in St. Petersburg. I don't want a failed state between us, but perhaps we can encourage something like the old Swiss canton system."

The Estonian ambassador snapped, "Why should we let you have a say in the administration of St. Petersburg? You are hundreds of kilometers away!"

Boris looked at him with disgust on his face, and contempt shaded his voice when he answered. "I only involve myself because of the suffering Viktor has already inflicted, you little rat. His forces have not crossed my borders. But I know my history. I know what a threat he could become. I would rather fight him with allies now, but if I'm going to, it is not to divide what was until a couple of years ago a stable area. Military empire always finds itself on rocky shores, it seems to me."

The Swede grinned openly at the final sentence. Major Nyland's face twitched, suppressing a slight smile. Both Finland and Sweden were based on a different concept to military empire. True, the Swedes were empire building, but a trade empire. The Finns were an almost democratic confederation in most ways.

The Swede said, with a hint of humor, "You have the proposal already written up, don't you?"

"Yup," Boris said, and pulled out a sheaf of papers, passing the copies round the table. Calmly, he said, "I will consider the changes you propose, but this is my concept of what is needed. I suggest you talk amongst yourselves." Looking around the table, focusing on the Estonian in particular, he finished by stating, "The Finns and the Estonians came to me for help. Don't try and dictate to me the terms on which I will help."

<<<>>>

His proposal had undergone some modification. Like himself, the Finns were more concerned with refugees and harassment from the expansionist Viktor. The Estonians had demanded a strip of land, including a large proportion of the cleared farmlands closest to their current borders. The Finns had grudgingly accepted so long as the Estonian borders moved no farther north, only east.

That would still leave at least a seventy-five kilometer buffer around St. Petersburg, and there was forested land and reverted farmland that could be used by the new realm. Their grudging acceptance made Boris suspicious of their motives. Still, it was an agreement he could live with, assuming everyone held to it.

"What is worrying you, Love?" Janna asked him, flicking her long, braided red hair.

"I wish we had a better feel for the Estonians. The Finns have a traditional hatred of Russians, but since the Fall, it has been exactly that. Tradition, not something they would act on, especially against us." Boris was worried. He was sure that with the abuse Viktor's people had faced, the mythological short victorious war was possible.

But he wasn't counting on it. He had planned for a three to six-year war and was using it to expand his military forces. The fortunate capture of that town, with supplies, to the south, had helped. There had been more there than Danislav's estimates.

Still, something was bugging him about the Estonians. Janna just nodded calmly and said, "I'll get some of my people onto it tomorrow. At least we should get some more information by the time our force reaches the edge of lands Viktor controls." She stopped and pointedly removed the sash of the robe she was wearing. "Now, come to bed. I'm sure I can think of something to take your mind off the worry."

Boris smiled and reached for the buttons on his shirt as he followed his love's instructions.

CHAPTER EIGHT

Two weeks later, New Romanovka was a picture of organized chaos. There were a total of five regiments—one more than Boris had planned for. A large number of mercenaries Boris had known ended up settling in Arkhangelsk after the Fall. With the resources he had made available to assist them, they had ended up considering him their effective commander, as did their children today.

Somehow, their town council figured out that Boris was going on campaign. Boris would have preferred for their forces to stay in place. Instead, he received an entire regiment from their paramilitary policing force. They kept telling him they were under his command. They wanted to show their determination to be part of his realm.

To be honest, despite the manufacturing he had set up with them, he never wanted them to integrate into his realm. That choice was now taken away from him. They were making a statement to anyone who could see that they were a part of his domain. He wanted to protect the Romanovkan people more than anything. Providing a base for Bethany Anne to return to was a close second. Creating a kingdom or an empire was not his goal.

As Janna had put it, he was a leader worth following. People would choose to follow him even if he tried to set them up as an independent realm.

Boris had shown a concern few leaders had after the Fall. Rather than hoard resources to those he was already protecting, he had spent resources, time, and effort to settle people across a large area. To secure that area, and to secure the machinery and factories that would be needed and move them to a place they would be useful. With that forethought and Lilith's help, he had made their survival in these times easier in his domain.

The new crop types that self-fortified made his people healthier and probably more populous than almost every other area on the planet. Akio's Japan would be the only place that was better off than his realm. Lilith's crops allowed more time for education by outcompeting weeds. They also produced higher volumes of grain.

All this resulted in the foundations for an education system. Children were not needed to pick the weeds out of the field. That freed them for school. The food surplus that the improved grains provided gave adults the freedom to pursue other tasks than farming and hunting—like teaching, for instance.

Those children who excelled in school could eventually study under scientists, mechanics, and Lilith. Boris had made special trips to 'rescue' many of the scientists and mechanics from areas that were hardest hit. It was the last time he had used the pods, before today.

If Boris were honest, the Arkhangelsk troops would be a great boon. They had a focus on house to house fighting in their training that no other unit did. They even trained to clear buildings from the top down. With his shuttles, they would be able to put those methodologies into practice.

Still, it had thrown his logistics into chaos. Adding around two thousand troops to his force was not a simple thing. Even with the extra logistics specialists they had sent, Boris had to bring in the additional supplies above what he had already collected. It would delay his departure by at least a week. He would still send the first two regiments, his regulars, to the border.

For the rest, he needed to get the supplies organized before he would be happy moving them, and he didn't want to run the two militia regiments and the Arkhangelsk troops independently. While they would be a boon assaulting St. Petersburg or defending any fortifications, they could be vulnerable on the march.

They had limited training in forests and on the plains. He also wanted to give them time to familiarize with the AK-74Ms he was equipping them with. While only slight variations on the AK-74, the improved grenade launchers that could be attached to their barrels were critical to his decision.

He decided to visit the training range. At least Mark was the leader of the St. Petersburg force. The son of one of the leaders of the mercs who had initially settled Arkhangelsk, he had trained with Boris's regulars. He knew how they operated.

Mark spotted Boris's approach and came out to meet him.

"How goes the training?" Boris asked the stoic man.

Mark looked much like his father. A stocky five-foot-eleven, he was in many ways like a nephew to Boris. While training had been offered to many of the Arkhangelsk officer candidates that met his standards, Mark was one of the few Boris had requested. He excelled in the training and his official position. He was currently the third most senior military figure in Arkhangelsk.

"The men were a little cautious at first. You know the M's grenade launcher adds a different flight profile to the basic 74's rifle grenade. I think they are getting the hang of it now, though," Mark said confidently. "I think that they will be confident with their new weapons once we head out. I appreciate the thought. A better weapon is always a boon." The gratitude in his voice was clear.

Boris shrugged and said, "What is the point of keeping something I have a surplus of away from a trusted ally? I wouldn't offer it to the Estonians. Too much risk of it being captured enroute. Besides, there is something fishy going on with them. They are more concerned about expansion than the threat. I'm worried there is something under the surface there. Janna has sent a family team that knows the southern dialect to investigate." Boris' tone had turned grim. He'd also sent a group of ten Werewolves to shadow the Estonian forces in wolf form and report on their movements

The roadmap of history showed that the current circumstances were ripe for betrayal. Social upheaval, combined with the small territories and the competition for resources, would push people to think of strange alliances. Similar alliances riddled both the Napoleonic era and the post-Roman era.

Still, Viktor needed to be removed.

Boris had to admit he was more confident of doing that with the Arkhangelsk regiment than without them.

CHAPTER NINE

It had taken six weeks, a time frame the trench diggers of World War One would have been proud of, but Olaf had his forward base complete. The nearby woods had sacrificed a significant amount of timber, but his operational headquarters was as good as they were likely to build.

Dug-in bunkers with overlapping fields of fire on three sides, nine of them, covered the large hill. Each had attached dugouts as sleeping quarters. One was close to the stream that ran along the base of the hill and had a well excavated into that bunker's center. This gave the base as secure a water supply as Olaf and his troops could hope for.

The Militias had been a great help in building the base. Used to creating housing, they had the skills needed to dig in the bunkers. They had only needed to take extra care lifting the turf. Most farmhouses in Boris's realm were dug into the ground for cooler, indoor conditions in summer and warmer households in winter. It also helped with the very short nights of summer. People still needed to sleep.

They wouldn't have been able to build it without the help of the shuttle. It seemed plebian to use it to haul split logs, but it enabled them to dig in their bunkers with logs split lengthwise on the logging site. This avoided leaving a trail to the base.

Now, his troops were secure, Olaf could start scanning the region to the west. With the two weeks of travel to the site of the forward base, they were near the old Belarusian border. Without the shuttle, they were at least three weeks on a bicycle from New Romanovka to the southwest of the town.

"Headquarters, assemble. We are going to mount up in the shuttle and scan the surrounding region for energy signals. Every theory of the weapon, from both the scientists and Lilith, state it has to give off a large energy signature. Unless it's on something like a nuclear-powered tank, which we should be able to track as well, it has to emit an etheric or dimensional energy signature.

"If it seems viable, we will raid the site to capture the weapon, so pack heavy. Otherwise, we return. Then, leaving a company on site to protect our forward base, the rest will equip for travel and mount a raid in force. Either way, we will leave a squad of Were volunteers on site to observe and report along the line of advance."

"Major Petrova, you will have command of the forward base. In the unlikely event communications are lost with the shuttle, you are to report the event to New Romanovka and move in on the last reported location."

The Major nodded unhappily at that. Although Olaf would have twenty-four people on the shuttle, if it was taken out, she didn't want to be the one to tell Boris and Janna. Someone would have to, though.

"Sir, I must request that someone else lead the scouting expedition, again. I know that you wish to be there, and that you believe that seeing the landscape we may need to fight across in person is important. But..." She paused and took a deep breath. "Boris is sure to be furious if you die on a scouting mission. In fact, it is arguable that neither you nor I should go on the first flight to assess an unknown threat that *could* take out the shuttle scanning for it."

Olaf grimaced, but held firm. "The risk is minimal at worst. The advantage knowing the terrain for myself is too great. Pictures and verbal reports only go so far. We have scanned the area between the town and here. We've talked to local farmers. There is only one force that any of the farmers have seen, and it came from the west.

"Out of all the countries with a propensity for weapons research, the only one that makes any sense is Belarus. The Russians would have placed such research in western Siberia, well away from any enemy. Politically, it is the one that seems to fit the type of country that the Forsaken preferred. If we don't find anything by the time we are scanning and searching a hundred kilometers west of Minsk, we'll have to re-think. But for now, we're doing exactly what my father ordered. I need to be there to judge if any raid is an acceptable risk and to lead the attack if it is. It is what my father would do." Olaf knew that to gain the full respect of the Weres, he needed to lead from the front when he could to do that. Without the support of the shifter community, he would never rule Arkangelsk Palden.

More than that, he needed to lead from the front for himself. He needed to feel the crash of battle around him. Both his mother and father had, and he could do no less, not if he was to rule as well as they had. He needed to know what his soldiers faced.

Discontented fear rumbled through the ranks of the officers, but Olaf silenced it with a glare. "Besides, the weapon only seems to ravage wood and flesh. Inside the alloy hull of the shuttle, we should be safe from it," he finished confidently.

With that, he said, "I leave in thirty minutes. Those designated troops need to be on the shuttle or be left behind."

<<<>>>

The shuttle was now halfway through sweeping a hundred and fifty kilometer radius around the highway where it crossed the old Belarusian border. The first sweep, scanning a seventy five kilometer radius, had picked up nothing.

Olaf was also miffed by how packed the pod was. With its engines, it didn't have a weight limit. So, Major Petrova had reinforced his planned troop to a platoon. The extra eleven women had been picked by her from the volunteers in her own company. It would reduce her average squad strength, but give her peace of mind. He could hardly refuse it without looking reckless. It made disembarking a little more awkward. An extra five minutes checking showed they could still exit the cargo bay at speed.

Olaf struggled with the so-called headquarters section. Now that it was reinforced, it was impossible to disguise the nature of the unit from him. All the reinforcements were shooters, and six of them were Weres. He hated to think what that would do to the efficiency of the unit, all to give him bodyguards. He hated the concept. He had yet to prove he was of enough worth to the people to deserve such.

It was all because his father had proved to be a good leader and feared any harm coming to his firstborn. How he wanted to be just an officer in the military. He didn't care if he was militia, reserve or regular.

He just wanted to be normal.

Then one of the sensors dinged. He looked at the repeater plot and frowned. Gazing at the pilot, he said, "What is that, Vlad?"

"It is similar to the first generation, two-man pod signature. I am breaking the sweep pattern to investigate. Reporting signature location to the base," Vlad answered in a detached voice.

As they got closer, Olaf saw the signature grow and peak. "Evasive!" he yelled, but Vlad was already jinking the craft across the three dimensions available in a complicated maneuver. A bright red arc, like lightning, flashed past the shuttle. Streamers reached out for it, but Vlad had generated a miss.

"Get a hill between us and that weapon!" Boris yelled. The pilot nodded absently and dove toward the ground. Unfortunately, the maneuver slowed the shuttle down as it passed the hilltop they wanted to land behind. The shuttle shuddered as something struck it.

Red streamers arced through the hull of the ship. There were screams of pain in the rear compartment, and G-forces suddenly took effect as the engine was hit.

"Brace!" the pilot yelled.

Olaf hoped everyone in the back had something to brace against. The shuttle bucked and heaved as the pilot used the emergency jets to slow the descent and the airspeed, as well as lift the nose to soften the impact.

Olaf was buffeted and bludgeoned as the shuttle hit the ground. He could feel it start to spin as it slowed. Hard bumps could be felt as the shuttle hit trees, but finally, the shuttle slowed to a stop.

"Evacuate!" Olaf called out as he ripped the belt loose and rose from his seat.

When he glanced at the back, he could see four people operating the emergency exits. The shuttle compartment was a picture of chaos. Blood and injuries were obvious on about half the troops in the rear.

He loosened his pack from the webbing it was in behind his seat and slung it, then turned to Vlad. He was wincing as he rose from the pilot's chair. Olaf helped him into the cargo compartment where another passenger took him from Olaf and towards the now open exits.

After grabbing the pilot's pack, he slung it over his chest. It had a dozen doses of the nanite recovery shots that Lilith was restricting production of due to the damage she was afraid they were doing to human DNA.

Boris made his way to the rear of the compartment, ripping open the emergency hatches as he went. There couldn't be more than a handful of kilometers between where they had crashed and where the weapon had fired from. "Salvage everything you can!" he shouted at those who were coming back into the compartment. He moved to one of the exits.

His heart was pounding. Others seemed to be moving too slowly as he stepped past them to see through the exit. After seeing the path of destruction, he scanned the surrounding terrain. Lightly wooded hills surrounded the crash site, and there was a clear furrow to the crash site. It would be easy enough to spot from a hilltop.

"Stretcher the badly wounded and the dead," Olaf ordered.

With firm commands, the troops started organizing the evacuation of the site. He pulled a compass from a side pocket in his pack.

Pointing to the northwest, he said "Start moving to the northwest. We need to start moving. I have to set the engine to blow." He struggled to the engine box at the back of the hull. The walking wounded and uninjured flowed past him, in and out, as they removed what could be taken from the shuttle.

He considered the possibility of removing the railguns from the turret on the roof of the hull, but remembered how involved the process was. It would take hours. Hours in which they could be pinpointed and attacked again. His troops were more critical than salvaging even those powerful weapons.

Cutting his hand, he placed it on a keypad at the back of the etheric reactor. He jerked as a small, red ark slashed into him. It shredded the right arm of his field uniform, disintegrating it and leaving charred edges where it struck. Still, the pad powered up as his blood dripped onto it and confirmed when he punched in 5400 seconds into the panel.

He had ninety minutes to get everyone out of the blast radius of about half a mile.

"Come on, soldiers. Move, move, move!" he yelled, grabbing equipment from nearby lockers and throwing it at his men as they approached.

The first time he did it, the soldier was startled. The second time, the soldier was ready. Within a minute, other officers were following his example. Within five, they were clear of the shuttle. An enterprising sergeant had taken the expedient of having a pair of Weres rip the pair of medium railguns off the turret. They would either work or not.

Within twenty minutes of the crash, the last of the group was moving out to catch up with the heavily laden troops in front of them. Some supplies had been abandoned at the shuttle. The self-destruct would make sure it was of no use to the enemy.

The sun was already starting to set. They were in hostile territory and had to find a place to rest, assess the wounded, and bury their dead. But first, they had to get clear of the crash site.

<<<>>>

When night fell, the cold fell quickly with it. According to the injured navigator and the map, they were marching towards the rocky hills to the north-west. Olaf was busy, hauling three packs and two of the dead. Both were from the humans in his bodyguard.

Nearly everyone was injured to one level or another, but there was one dead Were and six people that were hurt badly enough they needed to be carried on a stretcher. Another five stretchers were loaded down as heavily as possible with supplies. Despite all the trials they faced with their situation, they were making good time. Olaf had estimated the edge of the woods were three kilometers from the crash site.

They were approaching that edge before the shuttle self-destructed. Olaf picked up the pace, knowing it would be best if they were past the woods and up in the hills, behind a ridgeline, when it went off.

There were groans and huffs as he pushed the pace, but no-one complained. Those on stretchers had been given a dose of the charged healing nanites and were all stable, despite the movement.

Vlad was the only person genuinely struggling with the pace, but he didn't complain either. If anything, his fear was pushing him through the pain. He knew, far better than the troops, the radii of destruction for the self-destruct. He had some nanite support to interface with the shuttle controls. His limp had been gone within the first half hour. However, like nearly half the pilots, he'd never wanted a 'full' package.

He was regretting that decision now.

They were clear of the zone of direct effect, but until they had a ridgeline between them and the detonation, he wouldn't be happy. The indirect effects could be unpredictable. Usually, the blast blew outward and then in like any other, preventing the spread of the destruction beyond about a two-mile radius. There may be a hundred-foot circle of black glass at the crash site. There was a chance that a damaged unit would have a longer blast duration.

Considering his shuttle had been ripped from the sky by that weapon, and that he'd lost all the etheric engine controls, he was willing to bet the unit was damaged. That could mean a longer blast time, and a wider area of destruction as the blast winds pushed more debris for longer.

"Ten minutes!" Olaf shouted as he pushed the speed up another notch. They were climbing a hill and should reach the top in five minutes with the pace he was setting.

They made it over the ridge, and Olaf allowed a rest as everyone took in water and a few of the Weres opened ration bars. Olaf put down his load and took out his entrenching tool. Here was far enough to carry the dead. He started carefully cutting the turf. A few of the older Weres rose and headed down the hill to find some rocks for markers. Really, it was a bit of a toss-up between moving on with the bodies or burying them there.

Leaving them to be destroyed by the blast had been too disrespectful for Olaf. It was possible that it wasn't the battle-wise decision, and maybe it would improve the enemies chance of tracking them if there was enough of a trace to follow after the blast.

Either way, it was still the right and respectful decision to make. Besides, while the digging was going on...

Everything paused as the sound of the earth-shattering explosion hit them. Even at that range, sheltered by a hill, the boom of a catastrophically failing etheric reactor was impressive. The shaking of the earth as the shock wave passed was less so. Most of the energy would be directed up, even with the containment of the alloy hull.

"Andre, Richard, test those railguns. Aim for the blast site. Breaking it up will make investigating harder," Olaf ordered. He'd known about half of his bodyguards most of his life. He was more comfortable going by first name with them.

An *Amazon* and two of his bodyguards were the dead. Nestor, he knew, but he'd needed dog tags to identify the others. Marina and Timothy. He bowed his head, anger and grief mixing. If he'd not been so confident in the security of the shuttle, maybe this wouldn't have happened.

Of course, then it could have happened to others. No-one had expected someone on the planet to have a weapon that could take out a shuttle. At least not outside of Japan. Any other officer he could have sent would have only had a squad with them. Their chances of survival—even if they had taken no casualties—would have been lower still.

It had been the right choice to come. Or at least the best option available.

There was a single *whipcrack* from the hilltop as one of the railguns fired.

The tears of grief and regret flowed down his face as he dug the grave. Slowly, others started to help him. Within half an hour, they had it as deep as it would go, about four feet.

Even with all their technology, and even relative to life before the Fall, particular injuries were truly fatal. A crushed skull. A charred hole through the chest. A bolt of energy through the eye. *At least it would have been quick*, Olaf consoled himself.

He carefully placed each body into the battlefield grave. Anatoly, one of the Weres, handed him a hip flask of vodka. Nodding, Olaf carefully poured some over each corpse's lips. They would reach Valhalla with a drink on their breath.

Then he threw the first spadeful of dirt into each grave before letting others complete the task.

He saluted as the three rocks were placed to mark the graves, the earth was stomped back into place and the turf put back over to hide them from casual sight.

Olaf would forever remember this moment as the moment he learned a core soldier's truth. That loss and grief are at the center of war. He was coming to realize fast that glory was no balance to them.

He took a swig of the vodka before he handed it back to Anatoly, who took a swig himself before he put it away in his gear.

Olaf made an oath that moment. He couldn't stop people dying to protect him because of who his father was, whether it was out of fear or respect, but he would become a man worthy of any who died for him.

One of the railguns was working. The other would still have to be lugged with them. Olaf would not let it fall into the enemy's hands. For now, carrying it was better than slagging it with one of his few thermite grenades.

He had a feeling he might be happy for every weapon he had.

It was why the only weapon he'd left with the soldiers to arrive at Valhalla with had been their Tomahawks.

He knew they'd understand when the doorkeeper asked why they were so poorly armed.

Their comrades would put their other arms to good use.

<<<>>>

They marched through the night, towards the northwest. Although they needed to head back to the initial site soon, first they needed to find somewhere where the wounded and a few guards could hole up. Even with the single dose of nanites he'd given them, broken bones and damaged spines took time to heal. Especially since they'd been forced to march so far before seeing to the wounds properly.

Shortly before dawn, one of the two Werewolves Olaf had sent out to scout returned. They had found a copse of trees that was large enough to conceal the group. With watchers on a nearby hill, they would be warned of any approach.

Once they were down, and most of the troops were resting, Olaf cursed himself. Although he had sent a transmission of the enemy's location, he had failed to transmit his group's survival.

Now he had no means to. Considering that fact, he took the good with the bad. At least he wouldn't have to deal with his father's immediate temper, nor were additional shuttles likely to be sent. They were too valuable to use another.

Too valuable to lose another.

CHAPTER TEN

It had been two days since Olaf's shuttle had registered the self-destruct with Lilith. They had hoped for more information before this meeting, but none had arrived. Lilith concluded her initial report.

"The engine of Shuttle 0009 was restarted after failure by nanites holding the signature of Olaf. They reported high etheric reserves that would not have been present if the body had suffered significant damage. Indeed, there was a residual energy higher than his average over the last twelve months," Lilith reported to Boris in an analytical tone.

Boris smashed his fist down. "I don't care. I'm moving south to take command of the force under Major Petrova currently. The situation down there is a higher risk than we initially assessed. They need someone with more seasoning."

Paul raised an eyebrow at the outburst, but said nothing. Janna, however, was shaking her head vehemently.

"No, Boris. Danislav doesn't have the command experience for a five-regiment force. Worse, he's never been seen by the Pack as an Alpha. He has the strength for it, but the perception is he's always been your second. He'd have challenges for command within a day of news arriving with the rest of the force. The twins are too junior. I need to stay here until one of them gets back anyway.

"A divided command is the last thing we need there, and I can only guarantee the Arkhangelsk Regiment and Vilosty's regulars would accept him in command. Tolstov is ambitious, if loyal personally to you. The militia regiments could choose to place themselves under his command if Tolstov divides the command. His reputation as a commander is Danislav's equal," Janna said in a forceful, but analytical, tone.

"Both of them knowing that Olaf is missing or dead is the only reason you would command the South. Tolstov would look at it as the position of heir and second in command of the military being up for grabs," She finished in a disgusted tone.

"We have three other children," Boris said diffidently.

Paul snorted and said, "The twins aren't taken seriously by the populace, Boris. Hell, I'm not sure either of them would want your job. They would have to become 'proper.' As for Fiona," he paused and extended his palm flat, then shifted it from side to side, "I don't know if she'd come back. She's already the Mongolian pack's second in command. That position makes her heir to the civil leadership since the Fall, too. Her renown is greater than anyone else in a position to claim heir if Olaf dies. And even if she did take the position, who would replace her in Mongolia? Her departure could open the door to the Sacred Clan. We know they're still active."

Paul's voice held concern, with a touch of dread. As if he had already found a solution and didn't like it.

Lilith stated, "All indications are that Olaf is alive. The members of the bodyguard would have put in their code before the self-destruct, even if they used his nanites after catastrophic damage to his body. Only he knew the family nanites required no code."

Continuing, somewhat cheerfully, "If he succeeds without the presence of a currently accepted military better, the projections of his prestige gain are, in fact, better than before the crash. There are too many imponderables to give any estimate of success. We don't know what he could face."

Paul's face fell at the words 'currently accepted military better'.

He knew he was considered an analyst and REMF. He hadn't even been on a patrol in twenty years. Alecta had felt when the sniper's bullet creased his skull, or so she claimed. When he came to, he found out she'd had to be restrained. When she was more than a hundred kilometers distant.

If he didn't offer, Boris wouldn't even consider sending him. The problem with that was Boris would be frozen from indecision. He needed all his mind on the St Petersburg operation if he was to do the best there.

Paul grimaced internally, then said with an open grin on his face, "That only gives you one choice, boss. With what Lilith has just said, I'm your best option. Petrova's a hell of a combat commander. She can keep me from making stupid mistakes. I have the experience, both operationally and from heading analysis and assessment, to avoid the worst mistakes as we move in." He finished with a wink

"Alecta won't like it, but it's a command, not a frontline slot like Captain. I won't be breaking my word to her," Paul said.

Janna hid a smile as she said, "She may carry through with her threat and travel with you. She has Boris's word she could if you ever took up a command."

Paul only shrugged. He was half certain she would. He wasn't happy about it, but it was the best answer among a load of shitty solutions.

Boris looked at Paul as if studying his face. He almost didn't recognize the man. Gone was the serious professional, back was the joking warrior. Paul timed his final line perfectly.

"Besides, I have to back a play I've been suggesting for years.

I'll bet you that bottle of Glenfiddich that I've been keeping that your boy has everything sorted before we get there."

Boris had to smile at that. They'd been using a bottle of that whiskey for the better part of sixty years on bets they were sure they couldn't lose. The old Paul was back, and that was worth a lot. That he was willing to go back in the field meant much. And in the post-Fall world, a madman in command wasn't the liability it would once have been.

Especially since Boris and every officer in his forces knew he could be serious and was highly capable.

"Very well," Boris said as he rose and walked over to his friend. Kissing him on both cheeks and pulling him into a bear hug, he whispered to his friend, "It is good to have you all the way back."

Paul answered back as quietly, "It's good to be back. Now, let go of me before your wife or mine starts thinking there's something funny going on, you ugly fuck."

Despite the situation, or perhaps because of it, Boris couldn't contain his laughter as he let Paul go.

CHAPTER ELEVEN

The next morning Boris led the remaining three regiments out. He was grim-faced but without the malaise or lack of confidence a man who thought his son was dead or soon would be carried with him.

It was more the grim certainty of one who knew the unpredictability of battle and that a loved one would soon be caught in one.

Meanwhile, Paul was hurrying to form a command squad of ten. He'd found a lieutenant for adjutant, pinching him from Boris before his friend left. There were two solid sergeants he could pull from their temporary clerical assignments. The rest he would have to draw from the New Romanovka militia.

There was a polite knock on his door, and he absently said, "Enter." A file landed on his desk, and he looked at it. Then, he saw the letters AKA after Corporal Martia Ilyushin. The name next to it was his wife's name. He swore. He had spent too much time in work if she'd managed to go through militia training and reach the rank of corporal without him noticing.

Even if her rifle scores were still marginal at best, she was rated expert at unarmed combat and Wereform combat. Also, expert with a pistol and master with a shotgun.

He asked a simple question, "When?"

"When you made the trip to Mongolia fifteen years ago. I knew you wouldn't stay away from the field forever. Janna knew I'd be a liability in the field, but knew I'd follow you if you went back. She insisted. It was either I do the training, or you'd be shuffled out of the military side. I knew if they pushed you out, you would feel useless. It would destroy the you that I loved."

He made a face at her and then seriously said to her, "The things we do for love."

She smiled back and shrugged. "It wasn't that bad. Besides, some of the pack were annoyed at my military service exemption, even if I was a scientist first. It calmed down some trouble that was building. Janna had been training me in Wereform combat for fifteen years already."

Alecta scowled and grumbled "And she can still knock me out whenever she tries."

Paul had to grin. The local militia rarely did long distance patrols, and she had been 'sent to Arkhangelsk to assist with rebuilding' often enough to cover for that. Her file said she was a qualified corporal and was signed off by Janna, so she was qualified whether he'd known or not. Leo would be back in a day or three, so the capital wouldn't be without 'family' to look after it.

"Half my squad volunteered to fill out your command squad, sir," she continued. In the regulars and reserves, familial interaction like this was frowned upon. No family member could sit on a promotion board, and every promotion outside of his own family had to be signed off on by Boris, above the rank of sergeant. Paul, Vilosty, and Tolstov signed off on promotions for Boris's kids.

Both Boris and Janna promoted as the forces increased. There was no-one more qualified for overall command of any force or realm than Boris unless—or until—Bethany Anne or Michael returned. Janna was the one who had managed the entire retrieval of academics of every stripe that enabled everyone to prosper in their realm. That showed her competence.

Tolstov was a wildcard in many ways. Supremely competent, but ambitious, he was afraid of both Boris and Janna. While Olaf was the clear heir, he'd make no threat to them. If they showed no weakness and Olaf was gone, he'd not make a move either. But if he saw a large opening?

Well, that was something else.

But he was too competent to exile, execute or remove without active treason. Besides, Paul was sure Janna had people inside his confidence who would act before he could achieve anything against her or Boris personally.

Eisenhower had to deal with both Patton and Montgomery. Boris and Janna only had Tolstov.

'Fraternization' was a crime of the past since the Fall. Rape was an entirely different matter, but with consensual relations, well, they needed every child that could be produced. If a woman had to be moved to other duties because of pregnancy, that was as respected a reason as a re-assignment for a lost limb. It took about a year for a limb to be regenerate and a person to get full use back out of it.

One of the sergeants Paul was pulling in for this op was just coming off maternity leave. The other was her husband. Their nine-month-old would be fostered with the militia. It was a frequent and respected situation.

"Well, get them to grab their gear. At least it will save me from having to go through the entire file stack," Paul said with no small relief. In many ways, it was the sergeants and lieutenant in his command group that were critical. The rest of the personel served there as messengers, in case radio was contra-indicated, and bodyguards. He trusted his wife to have chosen competent bodyguards for him.

"Yes, sir," she said, saluting and back in military formality.

"We have a long bike ride ahead of us," Paul said with a slightly pained expression. He missed the days of motorcycles and helicopters. And with the threat taking out a shuttle, another couldn't be risked outside the borders. Especially when they didn't know how the first shuttle had been disabled.

CHAPTER TWELVE

Olaf knew they were in trouble. With the risk of long-term effects, he didn't dare use another nanite dose unless it was an actual emergency, but he still had four men on stretchers. They had been forced to move twenty kilometers northwest, but he'd been able to send four Weres ahead, searching for caves along the line of advance.

It had taken a two-day march to find anything appropriate, and that had been used by humans recently. Humans with rifles, by the scent of gun cleaning oil. It was not particularly surprising. Belarus probably had hundreds of caches before the Fall, and upgrading outdated military equipment had been a specialty. Ammunition stockpiles more considerable than most nations would have, a natural offshoot of such industry.

Russia was so vast that even ten times the ammo caches would be so scattered that they could be lost far more easily. Russia's population density had been less than a quarter that of Belarus.

There could still be half million or more living in an area only slightly larger than the region Boris controlled. Perhaps higher considering almost half the country had been forested before the Fall. Hunting would have been a simpler task than in the West.

The only reason Boris had more than that many living under his rule was that he had gone out of his way to consolidate survivors. Few leaders had the forethought to do so, not that many leaders had survived the Fall.

So many governments were considered culpable with what had happened that the population had taken the fear and anger out on them. Toppling them. That had left few organized and recognized leaders to provide such support.

Belarus was not such a unified realm. Even if someone had started the process, it would take longer than a decade to complete it.

So, Olaf had to worry about who had used the cave. Were they nomads merely moving through, hunting and scavenging? Or were they a more organized, militaristic group? Were they coming back? Were they potential allies or definite foes?

Olaf was lost in thought as others set up camp around him. Several of the Weres had gone hunting. Hunting as a wolf would leave less trace, even if they had to walk back to the cave as a man carrying the kill.

They could all use the fresh meat, and it was worth the small risk of a fire. The cave opening was very defensible. Guard posts above and around that cave mouth would give any attacker hell. Fresh meat to supplement the rations would improve everyone's morale.

Everyone in Boris's realm was too used to thinking they could wipe the floor with any opponent. This time, they had been soundly defeated by an enemy, and it hit them hard.

Olaf needed some time to think. If he hadn't been reduced below twenty-five troopers by having to detach guards for the wounded, he would have been tempted to march towards the initial contact point. He just could not see a way to safely perform a scout and scoot against a force that may contain a Vampire with fewer than that.

If the Vampire abandoned all caution and caught a group of less than five alone, it was entirely possible it would wipe them out. Numbers, or possibly Olaf himself, would be needed to defend themselves against one of those, and the Forsaken were a plague outside Boris's lands in Eastern Europe. The Swedes were the other exception Olaf knew of.

Both realms treated Weres well. Weres could pinpoint the Vampires. Then assault groups could put them down, but not without casualties. After a Forsaken came within a hair's breadth of gaining control over Sweden, the people found a determination to clear their lands of the threat.

A threat that had been revealed when a Vampire had tried to manipulate the heir.

Rejuvenating her to youthful beauty had, in retrospect, been too obvious and a mistake. A Were had managed to reach her and explain what would become her choices. The cost her people would already be paying. They had come up with a successful plan to counter the Vampire, and that had been the end of that.

Olaf shook himself. He needed to focus on the now. His opposition was known to have a Vampire. That meant he needed to keep his troops in groups of no less than five, three teams forward, two available to fall back on or to move forward in support. With the dead, wounded, and the pilot, as well as those needed to guard the hurt he had barely twenty available.

That made his best option to patrol the space around the camp until the wounded recovered. See what was going on in the vicinity, be prepared to move. Where there was a Vampire, within days, there could be a passel of Nosferatu.

Olaf called in Anatoly. Together, they started organizing patrols —Two of eight, one of five with Olaf. That should be enough to take out single Vampires. If Nosferatu were contacted in numbers, they were to fall back. Away from the cave to a secondary rally point. Gunshots should be heard across the patrol range and would signal the other operating patrol to converge on the secondary rally point.

One patrol would remain in place in the cave at all times. The signal that they would use was a shot from the railgun. It made a distinctive report that no-one could mistake for anything else. It was also as good as they were likely to get in protecting the bottleneck cave entrance. It would go through multiple Nos at once, crippling or killing any the slug passed through.

Olaf fervently hoped that a Nos attack would not happen. He had heard stories from his father and Danislav about how relentless they could be. There were a couple of other facts about them that niggled in his mind. For instance, Danislav had mentioned a propensity to hunt down family members.

In some ways, that would make them a devastating threat to any resistance movement. Find the family, turn a kid even, and that family would be, one way or another, of limited threat.

It could backfire, though. Surviving members could be even more driven to wipe out the Vampire. Or they could be broken. Unable to survive, let alone be a continuing threat.

Olaf hoped that was not a regular tactic. It wasn't something the Forsaken knew about, according to the records Danislav had researched before the Fall. Boris had only noticed it in passing over centuries, and often the Forsaken were more focused on immediate effects.

That combined with the semi-control they could impose on those Nos they created themselves meant few, if any, would realize that factor.

Lilith theorized it was an effort by the nanocytes to wind back the mutations to a level allowing Nosferatu to take conscious control. Close relatives would give the nanocytes the data needed to reduce the mindlessness, potentially.

That was not to say they wouldn't target anything with blood to maintain the host. Just that a preference for relatives between targets in close vicinity.

Turn one, and it would go where the host remembered living if no control was placed on it, on a kind of autopilot. That increased the risk to family members if nothing distracted the Nos as well.

It might explain the empty villages that Were scouts had reported before they had found the cave, though. If that was a tactic being used, then that would explain the empty expanse. They had crossed several tracks that were overgrowing. Like the population that used them had only recently stopped using them.

The only place with recent human scents had been the hills, the region around the cave. If they were going to find anyone who they could obtain local conditions data from, it would be here or farther north by the look of things.

That was part of the reason he felt the need to patrol. Anatoly noticed his silence, and with the briefing the original bodyguard group had been given—that there was a Vampire in the area—put two and two together.

"Olaf, don't go borrowing trouble. No Vampire around would take Nosferatu lightly. They would cut into the food supply too quickly now. Fewer and warier humans since the Fall," Anatoly said, placing a hand on the older man's shoulder. He felt oddly paternal to his commander. He had much more experience in the field than Olaf.

Continuing, Anatoly stated, "You made the right choice taking the scanning mission yourself. I was thinking on it while we were searching for a signal or signature. Now that we have gone down, we still have enough supplies to stretch out to a month with some hunting. A smaller group would have been able to stretch that longer. However, they would have been forced to go to ground and hide. There are still enough here that we can scout. Look for information. Even fire up the shortwave radio in an emergency and contact base."

Olaf frowned. The shortwave radio would give off a noticeable signature if they activated it. Pinpointing with even older radio detection technology would be easy. Without reliable satellite coverage, it was the only option for distance transmission. On the other hand, if they found something vital they would have to risk it. Perhaps even bait a trap with the transmission?

Still, it was not an answer for the current situation. It was not an emergency, nor had his forces obtained information that was of strategic value. A welter of concern filled Olaf. He kept to himself for the night, planning patrol ranges and time out before heading back.

<<<>>>

It was his third day patrolling, and they were about to head back. They'd found a few places that showed and smelt of recent human activity. The smell of anyone in the area ahead of them should have been brought to their senses by the wind that was blowing towards them. Olaf called time.

Though they had found a tracking sign, the Weres had been universally thwarted in tracking anyone by scent. They kept encountering patches of strong 'woodlands' odor that had overwhelmed their sense of smell.

Olaf was reasonably sure the hide they had found a half mile back was a day old or less. Still, even in his other form, the human scents had been faint. They were the smells of people who were taking extra effort to smell like the environment. Rubbing dirt and strong-smelling plants over themselves.

They headed back to the camp, the wind at their back, relatively unconcerned. They had patrolled the area only hours before, and apart from the hide they had found, no new sign of other humans. None of the telltale Vampire scent on the wind.

Still, his patrol moved cautiously. Overconfidence in the

shuttle was what had gotten them into trouble in the first place. They were halfway back, and the breeze went still.

Olaf's nose twitched, as did Andre's. "Cover!" he shouted out the order. There was a human odor in the air now that the wind wasn't blowing it away from them. His patrol quickly dove behind rises, trees, and whatever else they could find. Olaf himself took cover behind a tree.

He heard rustles in the brush ahead that confirmed his suspicions.

"It would seem that we are at an impasse," a voice from the woods said. "We have all five of you located. A firefight was not what we had planned, but we will take it if that's all that is on offer."

Olaf thought quickly, then decided provocation was the best option if they were the enemy. "That's all you have! We will not surrender to a blood drinker's lackeys!" he shouted back. He loosened the straps on his patrol webbing, preparing to shift if he needed to.

However, he was not convinced they served the Vampire. He thought he'd be able to smell what Danislav described as 'old, off blood' on a Vampire's troops. Especially if it had kept to one lair for some time, as many did.

There was silence for a moment, then a snarling, feminine voice answered, "We have nothing to do with that bitch! Most of us are survivors of attempts to 'cleanse' our homes with some of her monsters." That sounded more like this Vampire was nearby and directing the Nosferatu. That was a small relief.

Olaf hesitated. If he took it at face value, then he risked looking like a credulous fool in any event. Either that or arousing their suspicions about his motives. "I guess it is a standoff then. I sure as hell can't trust that you are not working for the blood drinkers!"

There was a pause as that sunk into the listeners. Then a shout went out from one of Olaf's men. The flanking group of enemies was the action that broke Olaf into action. His webbing hit the ground, as did his rifle. He quickly shifted into his bear form. He was moving as he was changing. Shots rang out, but Olaf charged at an angle. He was faster than any known Were. People used to targeting regular bears, leading the target for a normal bear's speed, had no chance to hit him.

Quickly, he was through their lines. As he broke through, he passed two of the ambushing troops. One of them he smashed into the tree he was hiding behind. The man slid bonelessly down the trunk, unconscious or dead. The other bravely tried to line up a shot while standing directly in front of Olaf. The bear he now was pounded the ambusher into the ground before the bullet could be fired.

There were shouts of consternation. Perhaps the Belarusians had not heard of, believed, or encountered Weres before. But the confusion of a six or seven-hundred-pound animal charging through their lines distracted the best of them. Olaf's patrol consolidated behind a group of trees that covered them from both the flanking movement and those who had remained in original ambush positions.

Olaf would worry about the damage the transformation had done to his clothes later. His armor was specifically designed to fit his bear form when he changed. It was not as strong as his father's solid overlapping alloy plate armor, as it was made of the same cloth as the regular forces antiballistic armor. The pants were obliterated by the transformation. He had two spare pairs in his pack back at camp.

A bullet pounded into Olaf's body armor as he was distracted by his silly concerns. *'Get moving, make a plan!'* shouted Danislav's voice in Olaf's head.

The order echoed through his mind. Plan, yes. Find the woman who had answered back to him. Take her into his physical control. It was likely she was the leader. If not, she was second or third in command. A hostage that gave him a chance for negotiation

Bullets cracked past him as he moved from concealment to cover and back to concealment again, sniffing the air for the smell of a female human. He could smell two, but only one was close to the location where he had heard the words shouted from.

Moving through the dense underbrush as fast as he could, dodging trees, he circled to a position directly behind her. He slowed, the sound of his continued forward movement covered by the ambushing force crashing through the underbrush to find him. There were occasional cracks of single bullets being fired.

They were no longer passing near him, so Olaf continued forward. When he found the source of the scent, he saw a young woman flanked by an older man and what he could only call a boy. Charging forward he flung the older man into a tree with a mighty backhand from a single paw. Several bullets impacted against his armor, moving down until they were hitting his rear.

The nine-millimeter bullets were more of an annoyance than a serious threat to him. They wouldn't have threatened an ordinary bear, let alone a nanite enhanced Were of Boris's line. They did, however, make him angry.

A single swipe of his paw as he rounded on the enemy ripped the submachine gun from the boy's hands. The boy froze and gaped as Olaf then rose onto his back feet and, after reining in his anger, headbutted his opponent.

Swinging around, he turned his attention to the woman. He heard her gasp to his right, and as Olaf turned, he heard her try to escape through the brush. He was too close. She could not have dodged his charge had she been facing him. When he brought her to the ground from behind, it had been inevitable.

Under the weight of his bear form, she was unable to struggle.

As he shifted back, she struggled mightily beneath him. Despite the disorientation of the shift, he managed to block an attempt to kick him in the groin with his thigh.

"Wh-what are you?" she gasped.

Shrugging internally as he yanked one of her arms behind her, he answered in a growl, "I'm a bloody Werebear, you stupid little girl. New Romanovkan."

Struggling and spitting as he pulled her painfully to her feet, she said, "Ha, myth and legend, are you?"

Olaf dragged her backward, putting his free arm around her throat in a headlock. Once he was up against a tree, he yelled out. "I have one of you alive. I call for parlay."

More quietly he said, "Your life may not matter to you, but if they don't stop firing, I'll have to take them out before they harm my men. I cannot guarantee I can take out fifteen or twenty more men without killing them."

She struggled against his iron grip. He neither tightened nor loosened it. He loomed over her, and their eyes met. His were calm, almost reassuring. Hers were filled with a fiery fury.

Their wills clashed, but her fire melted against his calm certainty. When he said, "Fifteen more shots before I go after your men," Olaf felt her flinch.

Another crack sounded, "Fourteen."

Again, "Thirteen."

She wrenched her eyes from his and shouted, "Cease fire, but hold positions!"

Good to his word Olaf shouted out, "Cease fire!"

"What did you mean by a myth and a legend?" Olaf asked as all firing stopped.

"Werebears are simply a myth. New Romanovka is a legendary place. A place where technology remains despite the destruction of it throughout the rest of the world," she said, scorn in her voice.

"You felt me change from bear to man when I captured you. Surely, you felt the change in what was holding you, and I am as real as anyone. As for the other? Surely, if a myth has become flesh, you should consider that a legend is real as well."

"Fine, tell me where it is then. On a map of the world."

Olaf considered for a moment, then physically shrugged and said, "It's about two hundred kilometers south of Arkhangelsk. That city still stands, although Moscow is a wasteland. My father, Boris, is probably either pissed as hell at me or marching a response force to 'rescue me' right now." He finished in a musing tone.

"Wait, you are telling me that the group of yours isn't the entire force?" she asked in amazement.

"No," Olaf said, leaving it as that stark statement.

There was silence for a moment as she took the time to absorb both his statements. But a concern filled her. How much could she trust him? Then she saw her younger cousin stir.

Olaf hadn't killed him. He could have, quite easily, if he had been the bear. Then there was the fact that the bear had been wearing something. Armor, she presumed.

Meanwhile, Olaf was shifting his position. Placing his hostage to give him better cover. Shifting so his armor slid back into its human configuration. He could see two men approaching from his left and the boy gathering up weapons on his right.

"Stay in sight, please. I don't want to have to hurt someone else. I'll do whatever I have to in order to keep myself and my men safe!" Olaf yelled out.

"Let her go, boy," said the oldest of the soldiers. "If you don't, we will find a way to kill you slowly and painfully," he added in a menacing tone.

Olaf laughed contemptuously at the threat. There was a chance they could kill him quickly. He couldn't see a way for them to capture him and contain him for the time a 'slow and painful death' would take.

"Vassily, run!" Olaf bellowed. Vassily was a Werewolf and would know what he meant. There were shouts of consternation as a wolf broke from the cover the rest of his patrol had found. Shots rang out, and Olaf started counting down again.

"Twelve, eleven, ten, nine," Olaf hissed through gritted teeth.

"Cease Fire! Cease Fire!" the woman still trapped in his grasp yelled with a panicky undertone. She was more concerned about what Olaf would do to her men than what the personal consequences could be.

"Now, stay back. If you want to solve the situation, I suggest you lower your weapons. Holding your boss up without hurting her at all is getting to be tiresome. I can keep it up all day and night if necessary, but it would be a bother." He paused as one of the ambushing troops ignored him and started to circle, moving closer. He also heard four more men approaching from behind the tree.

He yanked his hold on his captive arm tight, causing her to gasp. "That means all of you, including the four behind me. In fact, why don't you drop your weapons and move around to where I can see all of you. Just so there's no further... misunderstandings."

The man trying to circle him froze.

A yell from Olaf's men in the trees came forward, "You okay, boss? Or should we make a pointed argument against approaching you?"

"I'm fine, but if there is another gunshot things could get messy," Olaf answered loudly.

Continuing to the group around him, he said in a reasonable tone, "Now, where was I? Oh, yes. Our transport was taken out a few days ago while we were scouting for a damned Vampire. Some weapon that looked like an arc of red lighting."

"Personally, I've been hoping for a peaceful contact with local partisans if there were any. From how determined you are, I'd have to guess that you are them. A Vampire's troops would have either shot us both already or tried to break contact to report the presence of someone like me to their boss," he finished.

Some of the men in front of him looked doubtful. However, three of the four behind him put down their weapons and circled round non-threateningly. Keeping their hands wide of their body until they were in clear view from the front.

"While we wait for the others to come to their senses, how about you give me your name. I am Olaf, son of Boris, who is viceroy of Bethany Anne of TQB in Russia after she left Earth," he said politely.

There was a hiss from the surrounding troops. One of the rifles came up, and Olaf rolled his eyes at the reaction. "The Queen Bitch should have cleaned the planet of the monstrosities before she left."

Olaf shrugged and said, "I wasn't born until *after* she left. However, according to the records, she was facing so much resistance from the governments of the time she had no choice. All you have to do is remember what happened after she left to see how insane they were."

One of his comrades grabbed the rifle, jerking it from the guerrilla's hands and said angrily, "Killing someone born after the devastation won't make a difference, Marik. Killing the son of someone with Boris's reputation would be insane. My father told me about his reputation, as did Stasia I don't feel like having everyone in a thirty-mile vicinity killed. I still have family."

"What if this guy is lying?" Marik answered

"Then Boris or his children will be on our side. They won't like someone playing on their reputation and word will reach them. He's not one of the bitches' soldiers. They wouldn't have tried to convince us this long. Too paranoid," the saner man answered.

He gave Olaf a vicious grin. That expression was quite eloquent. It said, 'I believe you, but if you are pulling a con...'

Continuing, he said, "These men are patrolling in less strength than hers ever have anyway. They also reacted faster and better. Showed more discipline."

"So, Stasia, are you willing to tell them to put down their

weapons, so I can put down my hostage and we can talk like civilized beings?" Olaf said somewhat lightly.

There was a snort from his arms, and the woman said, "I suppose we can at that. Put away your weapons, boys. If he had ill intentions, he could have carried them through by now."

"So, what are the challenges you have faced…" Olaf started.

<<<>>>

After discussing the problems they both faced, Olaf was scowling. He had a bigger issue than he feared. The only blessing was the Vampire, Raina, had no Weres willing to follow her. She had at least two subordinate Vampires and a platoon of Nosferatu. Unusually controllable Nos at that, from what he was hearing. He hoped that wasn't like the situations in the archives. The one that had taken Bethany Anne to deal with.

If it was, they could well be screwed.

On top of that, there was at least three hundred human infantry. Mostly people who were happy to raid and torture for Raina. She hadn't been a known player, according to the records Olaf had read. The only French Vampire of note had been called 'The Duke.'

Stasia was remarkably understanding, even respectful, of Olaf taking her hostage. He had done it to prevent any deaths on either side. "You were saving lives," she had said, rubbing her shoulder. A rueful smile flitted across her face, and she said, "Although I didn't think anyone could exert that much pressure on someone's arm without breaking something."

"I've been training people in unarmed combat for decades. It's something you learn, the point before you do permanent damage. I regret the necessity of my actions," Olaf answered her.

She gave him a forgiving smile and stroked her hand down his wrist. Softly, gently she said, "I understand. You were in part testing who we worked for and part trying to prevent any casualties on your side. Then you saw us as potential allies and did not want to harm us. I can respect the measures you took."

"Good," was Olaf's only response.

He was still formulating a plan that might give them a chance. He had to estimate the response time from his main force. He had a feeling that could be delayed. They needed to set watches on Raina's main base. She would have to send a response out if the battalion moved forward.

Waiting for a day or two after her forces were split to intercept the battalion would be the best opportunity to raid the main site. He needed to find out numbers, both of the partisans and Raina's forces.

But first, he'd have to convince these guerillas that it would be worth the risk, at least as a group. Possibly on an individual basis. They had no reason to trust him, so how could he manage that?

CHAPTER THIRTEEN

Boris found himself looking at the ruins of the village. The houses were destroyed, the people scattered. The fields had even been burnt, removing what forage value for the horses they would provide. He was shocked about it, to be honest. Burning the fields at this time of year would have been difficult.

Woodsmoke and turpentine filled the air over the shattered houses. Boris shook his head in disgust. It wasn't like a village could be rebuilt from this level of destruction quickly. The town Danislav had found earlier in the year had also been torched, but there were houses still standing. Repairing them and replacing the rooms had been all that was needed.

Given all that humanity had suffered over the last fifty years, the destruction sickened Boris. What was the point of it? On a tactical level, it was wasteful. Strategically, there was some sense behind it. History told Boris the logic his foe was using.

Viktor obviously planned to trade space for time and as an attempt to stretch Boris's logistical lines. It was the traditional Russian strategy, used in history against both invading Mongols from the East and any invaders from Europe to the west.

It also implied that Viktor would have left some of his troops to harass Boris's supply lines. Boris chose to deploy Tolstov's regiment along the logistics chain. It was a critical job, and one Tolstov could not reject. It also carried little glory. Boris could almost hear the man's teeth grinding when it was given to him.

Word of what had happened to Olaf was sure to have arrived with the logistics train by now. That sort of thing was not something someone could keep secret for long. Once Boris had agreed to continue in command of the northern campaign, Janna herself had spread the rumor.

At least that way they would know of any distortions creeping into the rumors they released.

Boris watched from his overlook on the crest of a hill. A company split off the two battalions that were clearing the region to sweep the village. Searching each building, making sure that it was not already being used as a base for enemy partisans.

Boris rose as there was a commotion. One of the squads in the street moved in on a building, prepared to move in to support their comrades already clearing it.

Soon, a half-dozen soot-covered survivors of the destruction of the village were frog-marched out of the hut. Boris could only imagine that they had been hiding in a cellar inside the building.

Then Boris winced as he heard a crash across the other side of the village. Turning, he saw the black cloud of ashy dust rise from the collapsing building. There were shouts as another two squads moved to aid their fellows that were trapped in the wreckage. Clearing anywhere house to house was always messy.

Clearing ruined villages were costing him casualties in injured, even if he doubted any of the buildings were substantial enough to kill anyone in their collapse.

His face took a grim cast for the hardliners as he approached the village to interview the prisoners. He hated risking his men's life and limb against these delaying tactics, but he had no choice. Underground storage places were all too common this far north. Even if the summers were far warmer and the winters shorter than the first few centuries of his life, high winter was still a time of bitter cold. In these troubled times, cellars also made far more sense as protection for critical stocks of food supplies.

After all, what was the point in surviving a raid only to starve to death? Who wanted to have to choose between their long-term survival and the starvation of their children? Their children who would not survive in this world without the protection of their parents.

These were questions Boris had once hoped only the people of his past would ask. That the people of his future would not need to ask them.

It was with a grim expression still on his face he moved towards the prisoners. Five of them cowered as he approached, the sixth looking defiantly at him, anger blazing in his eyes. Internally, Boris smiled at that. Anger was good for several reasons. Angry people rarely censored themselves and were often a good source of intelligence.

"Where were you?" the man yelled angrily, "where were you to stop the rolling atrocity our lives became? First, Viktor steals our daughters for his harem and the amusement of his soldiers. Then he takes the strongest of the young men away to serve his state. Finally, his troops move in to destroy our village for the good of the people, herding our neighbors like cattle towards St. Petersburg!"

Boris looked down at him, allowing some of his anger at being blamed to show in his eyes. "I received no messages. I'm only moving against Viktor now because he threatens the borders of a state that *asked* for help. How in the hells am I supposed to help those who need it if they do not have the balls to ask?" He ground out the question at the end through gritted teeth.

"Still, I will give you a choice. You can either aid my men, caring for any who are injured in the fight to come, or return to my lands, or you can die here and now. I will not leave potential enemies behind me. All I ask is for the numbers of those that came to destroy your village." Boris paused, weighing up his options.

That man would never make a good soldier. Perhaps one of the other five might, but people who waited to be saved and complained when it didn't happen weren't worth wasting time on beyond the information he could gain.

He judged the prisoners to be between thirty and forty years old. Four men and two women, laying testament to how many women had been taken from the town. After looking them all over, he said, "You have perhaps an hour before we leave this village to decide. Think about it," Boris said before turning away and moving towards the house that had collapsed on the other side of the village.

By the time he reached it, the fighters that had gone in to investigate had been pulled from the wreckage. Minor cuts and bruises and an injured ankle where one had fallen through the floor of the upper story. They'd been lucky this time.

And still, they had no choice but to continue operating in the manner they were. If his forces did not, they left themselves open to far more casualties from guerrilla warfare along the line of their advance.

One of the guards came up to Boris and told him that the prisoners had made their choices. Three were returning to his lands with the next prisoner movement. The other three were willing to help care for the injured.

One of the women had even been trained in nursing by her mother and grandmother. It was people willing to keep skills active that were the pebble against which tyranny stumbles. Boris simply had to make sure that he was there to break the back of the tyrant as it stumbled against his people.

<<<>>>

"Reports are still coming in from units on the far flanks," the intelligence officer said in a matter-of-fact tone, "but it appears that your initial impression is correct, sir. They are scorching the earth as they retreat, taking as many people as possible with them and leaving nothing that may provide us with any form of support."

"Idiots," Boris growled, "there is not a single state that can truly use the traditional Russian tactic effectively. Not in the North, at the very least. Some of the remnant states of China might be able to, but up here, no single state controls more than a three-hundred kilometer radius. That makes the destruction more wanton than tactical."

"Historically it has worked, sir. It slowed the Nazis advance in World War II. It held Napoleon at bay," The intelligence officer answered differently.

"And in both situations, there was both more depth and less importance placed on logistics by the enemy it was used against. With the possible threats we face to our logistics line, there is simply no way for them to effectively cut it. The largest group of troops that I can imagine them getting in behind us would be a company." Boris responded with the confidence of someone who had lived it.

"Our entire logistics chain travels at company strength and is at least as well-trained in combat as any of Viktor's units. Better, from our point of view, more than eighty percent of our troops have seen actual action. More than half the reserve and all the regulars." The intelligence officer replied coolly.

Boris just shook his head in disgust.

Once the war was over, he was going to have to spend more time, effort, and resources than he had planned on rebuilding just the homes and trackways that the vast majority of the population would need.

Turning to Danislav, Boris asked, "What is the schedule like?"

Danislav answered with a smile on his face, "We are running

at least four days ahead of schedule. The vanguard troops cleared the main line of advance efficiently, and your force crossed the border ahead of schedule. They are still ten or more days out from being in the region you designated for our forward operating and logistics base.

Boris grunted. He devoutly hoped that Janna would have the first intelligence on what the hell was going on in Estonia by then. There was something about the whole situation that made his shoulder blades itch. He'd experienced that feeling many times hunting Vampires, most often just before one of them got the drop on him.

"And Paul?" Boris inquired

"Janna reports Paul has arrived at the forward base. He is finishing the logistics organization for the march on the region Olaf disappeared in. He should be in range to send out scouts around the time we start digging in our own planned forward base. Being a smaller force, he plans on moving slower than you are pushing, scouting more comprehensively," Danislav answered.

Boris nodded at the answer. It was always better for a small force to avoid a forced march. It would give them the energy to dig in quickly or dodge out of the path of a larger enemy force.

Boris needed to move more quickly so he could tempt Viktor to do something stupid. Paul had no such need. In fact, Paul's biggest problem was an information deficit far greater than Boris's own.

"So, everything is moving as planned or better, is it?" Boris asked the staff surrounding him.

There was a collection of nodding heads from everyone except Danislav. His foster son knew exactly what Boris was implying.

"Send messages to all commanders to intensify scouting efforts. The last thing we need is a visit from Murphy. Now, while everything seems to be running well is the time he will make his presence felt. We will avoid it if we can and limit the damage done if we cannot," Boris said, ending the meeting.

There was a long march still ahead, and he needed to work on what the few villagers that had visited St. Petersburg were able to tell him about the occupied portions of the city. He was still thinking of an assault plan when he finally fell asleep.

<<<>>>

Paul sighed and scrubbed his face. A miasma of fear had met his arrival two days ago. Major Petrova had not been able to hide her terror when he arrived. She had been resigned to execution at best. Paul snorted.

No matter how angry Boris might have been, he would never have executed anyone for losing his son. Dismissed them from current and future service? Yes. Execute? Never. Given the circumstances of what had happened, he would not have even gone as far as dismissal or rank reduction.

When Olaf returned, he was likely to receive a stern dress-down on what behavior constituted an 'acceptable risk.' Paul would do his best to convince Boris not to take it too far.

After all, Olaf was only taking such risks because he had been held back so long by his father—probably. Being honest, what Olaf had done might have been the best option anyway.

At most, twenty-five—what was considered a 'normal' full shuttle load—had been sent without him being on board. They had crammed the shuttle tight to fit over thirty. Ten extra soldiers could make a big difference to people fighting rearguard actions and needing to use hit and run tactics.

A far bigger difference than the same ten would likely make for the heavy battalion that was at the base.

"Are our units prepped? Ready to move out in the morning?" he asked Major Petrova.

Bracing, she said, "Yes, sir. Everyone is ready for movement. A quarter of the artillery has been dug in, and teams of picked Weres and humans have started moving out. The flank-forward scouts moved out a half hour ago." She paused and looked at her watch. "The forward scouts should be moving now."

Paul nodded, "Good work."

He was glad that his troops had been dropped at the border by shuttle. Riding fourteen hours a day, it had taken two of those days to reach the base. They had needed a day to recover from the four-hundred-kilometer trip.

No army before the Fall had troops fit enough to perform such a feat without motorized transport. Only the fact that the Weres took the extra weight off the humans had allowed them to complete it.

He had made it clear to Petrova that she was his tactical deputy. They had a mission and there was little if any reliable intelligence on possible enemies on the route. There was no way that there was a force more than twice the size of his current unit in the region.

Not unless they had come from farther west than Janna believed likely. With all the civil wars in the region, a leader from Western Europe should have consolidated where there were more resources. If that area was even recovering yet.

Chances were that it had not. The heavier urbanization and larger populations would have been hit harder than anywhere in the east of Europe when the electric and transportation systems had been destroyed. Without shipments of oil, they could not have had a high survival rate.

Boris hadn't investigated farther than the western border of Belarus. He had seen enough devastation in his long life. He had no desire to see more, and the reports from Sweden had not been encouraging. They had been forced to close their borders to the south soon after the Fall.

It seemed unlikely from the reports they had received that any significant military force could have been built. There was too much recovery needed. For that, the people required police, agriculture, and trade. A military force was an expense they would not have the money or other resources to afford.

That left the potential of local forces. Belarus had been a dictatorship before the Fall. The civil war and chaos that enveloped it after the Fall had been something Boris had monitored. Eventually, the factions that split the country until it was left splintered with limited communication. Assuming the increased birthrates common after a war, the region they were to target could muster a force. Even a force large enough to be a threat to the one Paul commanded.

But how much of that force could be deployed? How vast was the region it drew on for recruits? These were the imponderables. Paul believed that it was unlikely to be as well equipped, but planned to face a force of equal size and equipment.

Belarus was always going to be a wildcard. They had been heavily involved in weapons research. Before the Fall they had also been a secretive dictatorship. Their primary export had been upgrades for older weapons systems—systems that major militaries considered obsolete.

If there was any group that might have found a way to power armored vehicles without access to oil, it was the Belarusians. Any method Lilith had come up with so far had limited their utility. But Lilith wasn't very military minded—someone like the Belarusians could have found a way.

With the shuttle being taken down by an unknown weapon, something they had not expected any weapon to be capable of doing, Paul had to be cautious of everything. They needed to be ready for anything.

There was a tap on his shoulder, and he turned to find his wife glaring at him.

"Stop that," she hissed angrily, but quietly. There was no-one left in the dugout room they were using but the two of them. Complete decorum wasn't necessary for her when she was taking the role of concerned wife. "You are overanalyzing things. You have the troops, and especially the Major, back in control of themselves. Back to just worrying about the enemy. It's not like there is a lot we can do about the lack of information. We have a mission. We need to complete it. Worrying about the maybes is not your job now. Acknowledge them and move on."

Paul looked at her and blinked. Alecta was right, and he was supposed to be the military man of the pair. Somehow, since the Fall, they had switched roles. He had become the analyst, the one looking at problems and possibilities. She had become a woman of action, looking for solutions in the real world rather than chasing abstract possibilities.

'Hell, in the last decade she has been on more active patrols than I have!' flitted through Paul's mind. Taking a deep breath, he pulled himself back from the panic that had been building.

He looked into her eyes and murmured, "How do you put up with me, dear?"

She stroked his arm lightly and shook her head with a slight smile. Paul knew she hated it when he said things like that. Alecta felt she had put him through as much, or more, grief than he had her. But simply speaking the words and seeing her smile allowed the stress, guilt, and strain to drain out of him.

"Come, love," Alecta said "Come to bed. We will not have much time for sleep soon enough. It's best if we don't short ourselves now. And if you have trouble getting to sleep, well, I am sure I can think of something..." She focused a smoldering gaze on him, then took his hand in her own.

A smile danced across his face as she pulled gently on his hand. Rising, he followed her across the room to the camp-beds set up in the corner. Indulging their desires would be awkward, but he was sure they could find a way to improvise.

CHAPTER FOURTEEN

Olaf was growing angry with the situation. For five days, he had been sending a pair—one of his men with one of the partisans—to the resistance leaders. There were only five resistance members left with his group. He did not want to move his camp without them knowing about additional neutral to friendly forces in the area.

The next ambush was unlikely to have a happy outcome for either side. They should be allies—they should at least be able to talk.

Olaf had suggested to Stasia that she head out with the next pair, but she had outright refused. Once everyone was clear, she had explained why.

"I cannot travel with too few people. While it's unlikely that they will be captured, it's not impossible. I know the meeting schedule. If I were to get captured by a surprise ambush, it would be a disaster," Stasia told him quietly.

Olaf looked at her disgustedly. Of course, they had organizational meetings. Without them, any efforts they made were mosquito bites. With some form of coordination, their efforts would have a lot greater effect.

It would have been good to know before he had scattered ten people across the region looking for her father with a message.

Scowling, Olaf said to her, "And you didn't mention this earlier? I understand not telling everyone, but why didn't you tell *me* earlier? I could have traveled with your group by myself. Or, we could have traveled as a combined force."

"It was not the best solution. My father… He's going to be angry you are even here and angry your people didn't arrive to help years ago," Stasia said, her face blazing with shame and humiliation at having to admit that. "Father is not rational on the issue. He resents that no-one has arrived to help. He was raised on tales of the mighty Russian empire and the clever but dangerous European nations. He's convinced they should have recovered decades ago, that the only reason Belarus is in such a state is that outsiders decided to abandon us."

Olaf could not stop himself. He snorted his disgust at the concept. Everywhere was smashed down by the Worst Day. The only exception he knew of was Japan. They had reacted as one would expect. They had closed down. Closed to everyone outside the home islands. They still talked to his father occasionally, but Boris felt it was best if they remained a mysterious bastion that others didn't even consider approaching.

"We were all suffering. It is only in the last year, or so my father started extending outside his initial declared lands. We started more than a thousand kilometers away. What was your father expecting? For us just to *know* the people in a region that distant needed help?" he ground out at her.

"It is ridiculous, I know. And now help has arrived. I'm simply not sure how he will react. I'm afraid that he will try to execute one of your men for the failure to help us earlier," she said grimly, "which would be insane, yes, but I'm not sure he *is* sane. It was ten years ago when all this started for us. My mother came home a monster and started by feeding on my brothers and sisters. If he hadn't been out with my oldest brother and me, training me to shoot, I would be dead. But it broke something in him. Something he cannot fix."

She sighed and continued, "I was the only one who saw what she had become. The hunger, rather than love or grief in her eyes when we returned home. I was the one who shot her between the eyes before they could even recover from the bloody sight we found. My brother has forgiven me, but even now I'm not sure father has." She looked at Boris with a grim face. "I knew something was wrong when I saw her licking blood from little Jakob's body."

A sob broke her composure before she pushed on, "She was not my mother anymore. She was a monster. Stories were already being told in the markets and villages we visited about such and about how to deal with them."

Olaf looked at her, startled. He wanted to wrap her protectively in his arms as he heard her tale. But, everything in her body language told him doing so was not a good idea. Her arms were outstretched as if pushing everything in the world away from her.

Softly, but intensely, he said, "You did the right thing. There was nothing you could have done to save your mother at that point. She was a monster. She was not who she once had been. She was an unsuccessful attempt by some Vampire to create another. When the turning fails, the victim becomes a hungry, vicious, eating machine. Many called them Nosferatu before the Fall. They lose any sense of what they had been."

Stasia looked confused, so Olaf continued. "Vampires are those that successfully change. They retain their intelligence and most of their memories. Often, the infection does change their personality, though. Nosferatu are walking appetites. Cunning, but not intelligent, and not even a shadow of their former selves remains. What you killed may have had the shell, the form, of your mother. However, your mother was already long gone."

Stasia stood there a moment, processing what he had just

explained to her. Then a pair of tears started traveling down her face. Olaf could not hold back any longer. In the darkness the world had become, people needed to comfort each other.

He reached forward and pulled her into a firm hug. At first, she stiffened at the intrusion into her space. Then, as his warmth and his understanding of the tragedy that had befallen her family enveloped her, she started quietly sobbing. He held her until the grief she had kept so long locked away flowed out in a torrent.

She had been afraid her mother had somehow chosen to become a monster. She had never grieved because of that, thinking the worst. However, knowing that the beast had instead stolen her mother's form and there was nothing truly left of her beauty and kindness by that point allowed Stasia to finally grieve for her.

<<<>>>

Once the grief had run its course, she had fallen into an exhausted doze. Olaf let her sleep, thinking about what she had said—she was not likely trusted by her father and perhaps some of the other resistance leaders. She was a leader herself. That meant enough to him. He trusted her. He hoped at least. Perhaps trust was not the right term. Respected might be better.

It would have to be enough to work on. She did not know where the Vampire based herself, but a half-dozen of the leaders she knew did. Olaf needed that information. He may well need the forces they commanded as well.

He needed to go to one of the leaders' meetings. He waited until after the evening meal before he brought it up again. They had to be getting close to the point where Major Petronova was nearing the borders of the Vampire's territory. They could lose the opportunity to act and cut the head from the snake if they did not move soon.

She could take this weapon and run if her force was defeated.

That was the last thing anyone, local or from New Romanovka, needed.

He had to admit the fact that she had shot the Nosferatu both impressed and concerned him. It impressed him because it showed, even at a young age, she had the necessary internal fortitude to do what was needed. It concerned him because it also showed that she may still react rather than thinking something through. To survive, he slowly admitted, it could be a necessary trait.

He put it to the side. It was a trait she seemed to have that he could account for. Finally, he reached a decision. Taking Stasia to the side, he said, "We need to move. Either your people will be with us or they won't. We have to hit their base when it's vulnerable. I cannot see a sensible strategist inviting an attack from Petronova's battalion. It would be suicide to expose it to such an attack unless they are far weaker than you have described."

"What do you mean?" Stasia asked, sounding confused. "A battalion is what, five hundred men? They only have three hundred or so."

Olaf rolled his eyes and looked at her, "They only have three hundred that you have encountered. I'm not criticizing you, but with ninety guerrillas on active operations, how many do you have recovering or doing other tasks?"

Stasia paused and stopped to think. Slowly she answered, "Maybe a hundred and fifty. Hunting, farming in a few hidden sites, scavenging. Maybe a few more."

Olaf nodded and then said, "And from what you've told me, you only hit them from the west. We have no idea how far east she operates. I have to assume she has at least another three hundred on that side of her lands. That leaves her with as many as another three hundred she can probably field in an emergency. So, let's say that there are two hundred too far out for her to consolidate. That leaves seven hundred she could send out. I guess if she goes personally, she'll leave fifty or so at the base.

"If she stays, I would estimate anywhere up to a hundred and fifty, including any Nosferatu she has maintained control of. If Raina is a typical Vampire, she will stay in the rear, but we can't count on that. In a careful assault, I would expect my force to be the equal of any sixty or seventy of the enemy. Your guerrilla forces should be at least equal to her soldiers. So, I need at least a hundred and fifty guerrillas to reinforce us if we assault her base. Otherwise, we will take too many casualties," he offered.

Stasia was thoughtfully looking at Olaf, then she shrugged and said, "There are more than ninety of us active at one time. Finding that many willing to join in an attack on the base may be pushing it. Then again, if we have long enough to gather them we can probably find as many as two hundred and fifty."

"And if we use distraction tactics to disperse them around the area surrounding the base, we can defeat them in detail, increasing our effective numbers and reducing theirs," Olaf finished.

Stasia sighed and nodded, "Very well. Get everyone ready to move in the morning. The next leadership meeting is in three days, and it's two days travel to the north-east."

Olaf nodded and started circulating among his troops. They would be ready to move at dawn.

CHAPTER FIFTEEN

The meeting place was, Olaf had to admit, a magnificently beautiful place. The smell of damp earth mixed with the spring's smells of budding trees and the sharp odor of fresh water from the stream next to it.

It still made Olaf an unhappy man. It was too closed in. If an enemy force got close enough, they could easily surround it and trap whoever was in the dell.

He was glad to see that they were not the first to arrive and had been happy to send a couple of Weres out to hunt for deer to cook for the meeting. He also set teams of five to watch the most vulnerable approaches. He was still incredibly nervous about it all. His watchers were having to trust individuals from the two groups they had met at the site for identifying friendlies.

There had been worse setups in history. Indeed, partisans in World War II had often been forced to rely on radio given time/date coordination methods with groups outside their cells. At least many of the guerrillas in the region knew some of the members of several other teams.

Not all the individual guerrillas would be coming, he had since learned. Many were sending just their leaders and a small bodyguard. Others were sending single voting representatives. Oskar, the leader of the small band that had arrived first, had glared at Stasia when Olaf had first told him about his minimum requirements.

"We can easily find four hundred fighters that will be interested in your proposal. That is not an issue. The issue is convincing us you can take out the tank the bitch has up and running," Oskar had told him. "Stasia was only talking about the unit her family leads. There are a dozen, maybe more, of a similar size in the region. Many of the representatives bring homing pigeons to these meetings. Getting a secure message for a meeting point to organize an assault on the base is not the issue. Assaulting their base past a damned tank that can incinerate any that get within a kilometer, that is the issue."

Olaf only shrugged and answered. "I have such a weapon. I can even give a demonstration of it if necessary, but that can wait for the meeting." He liked Oskar. An 'older' man of about fifty, he was five-foot-six and had a teak hardness about him. It was as if rather than being worn down by age and hardship, it had merely toughened him.

"So, you think an assault on the base is possible with my platoon leading the way?" he asked the guerrilla leader.

He had already shown those currently at the site his other form when Stasia had explained how five of his had disrupted and would have been able to take out her patrol of twenty-five. That they had managed to gain the upper hand after being ambushed.

"Not only possible, but if you can take out the tank, it's necessary. This long struggle needs to end for the people to recover. I'm ashamed to admit my family was part of the groups that pushed your kind—the Weres—out after the disasters. We blamed them. Perhaps if we had embraced them, we would not be in the situation now." There was a sad tinge of half-wonder in Oskar's voice as he spoke.

Olaf smiled, and gently patted the man on the shoulder. "Perhaps not, as well. It's possible that if this Raina had defeated the leaders of the packs, she would have subjugated them as well. She is a third or fourth generation Vampire at my best guess. If she is the third generation, few Weres would have risked fighting her. My father would have, as would my godfather or siblings, but we are of a different line to most." He looked off into the distance.

He had heard about the pogroms that had enveloped Eastern Europe after the Fall. Weres had suffered, though not as severely as the Vampires. His father estimated that in the first five years after the Fall, anywhere up to ninety percent of the active Vampires had been killed. But all the Weres had been pushed either east or west from those nations. Few had been killed, but in Romania, Latvia, Belarus, Serbia, and a few other nations, they had been forced out.

Boris wasn't furious about what had happened. He had seen it all before. The people had been afraid and had needed to take that fear out on one group or another. In some ways, it was better for the Weres and Vampires to be a target. Vampires are restricted in their travel habits. Weres are not. Once the fear had become evident to them, many had fled to the wilds and kept hidden. Others had lived in their animal forms. Whereas Vampires were dragged by mobs into the sun, killing them.

Not only that, it had driven many Weres to Boris's realm, bolstering the numbers there. The extra help with hunting had made it possible for him to rescue and provide for more refugees.

Still, given the general antipathy between Weres and Vampires after the Fall, it would have been just as likely that they would have been a boost to the guerrilla movement.

In the meantime, Olaf kept considering other plans. Other options with the potential forces that would be available to him. It was obvious that Oskar was tired of the conflict. It seemed likely that others would be, too. So long as it wasn't a suicide operation or one that was too high a risk, Olaf was more than willing to help them with it.

<<<>>>

The meeting was tense. Planning between groups often was. When Stasia had introduced Olaf, it got worse. At least half the partisan leaders were highly suspicious of any outside influence. Others were positioning themselves, either around Stasia or around the leader most hostile to the plan. That leader was her father, Andrev.

Olaf could see he was growing less and less reasonable. There was a glint of insanity in his eyes. Slowly, Olaf came to realize both the wisdom and the folly of being convinced not to wear a weapon or sidearm to this meeting. The wisdom was they probably would have attacked him by now if he had. The folly was they were going to attack him anyway.

When her father started a diatribe, Olaf could sense an imminent danger. "Here they come to 'rescue' us, to 'help' us after abandoning us for fifty years," the madman thundered. "We have a chance here to show them we do not need or want such help at so late a date. Screw them. We can find a way on our own."

There was a murmur of agreement from the crowd around and behind him as he paused. Despite the display of cooperation, others who held less strict views started edging away from the vehemence he was displaying. Physically distancing themselves from where the insanity was being presented.

"We need to send the message that we are independent of all would-be tyrants." Andrev's eyes narrowed like a coiled snake just before it struck, and Olaf hesitated for a moment. It was a moment too long. As fast as a serpent, Andrev drew his pistol and fired three shots at him. Before the echo from the final crack had finished, there was the hiss of a knife being pulled from a sheath and Andrev's eye sprouted a hilt. There was a brief expression of shock on his face.

In almost the same fragment of time, Andrev and Olaf collapsed to the ground. The only difference between them was that Olaf was still breathing.

"Gods be damned, that hurts," he gasped as he felt the pummeling his chest had taken and a burn from the side of his face where a bullet had grazed it.

Then his attention was drawn to a gurgling sound behind him. Twisting to his feet and turning towards the sound he groaned in pain. He spotted where it was coming from. Oskar had been hit by the bullet that had grazed Olaf's face. He had been standing on a rock towards the back of the crowd, watching.

Olaf recognized the sound. It was the familiar sound of a punctured lung as it struggled to inflate with every breath. Stumbling through the crowd, he scrabbled at the aid kit on his pouch, the one that contained a precious dose of nanites. It would take his platoon dose numbers to below fifty, even with the extras from the shuttle.

The crowd parted as he stumbled almost drunkenly towards the older man. The man who had been dreaming of life after the fighting. A tired anger burned through Olaf.

Oh, how he found himself hating conflict and war. He liked Oskar, and when he looked at the wound, he realized it was a large caliber round that had struck the old man. Giving up on opening it with clumsy hands, Olaf tore the first aid pouch from his belt. The Velcro made a ripping sound as it came loose. He dropped to his knees and dumped the contents of the bag next to Oskar.

Quickly sorting through it, hastened by the weakening gasps from Oskar, Olaf found what he was looking for. The bottle of nanite dose. Pouring some of it over the wound on the front, he waited.

Once he saw that nanites were doing their job, he turned the critically injured man to his side and started sprinkling them into the gaping wound on his back. Oskar was lucky not to have been killed instantly. If the injury had been further to the left, there would have been nothing Olaf could have done.

As it was, Olaf was sure a single dose wouldn't allow him to recover fully. The damage had been catastrophic. Without nanites, even with a full pre-Fall surgical team, Oskar would have almost certainly died. The wound on Oskar's back started to seal and fill in. Progress was slow. Olaf had been right. The damage was too much for a single dose of medical nanites.

Seeing the scalpel blade on the ground, Olaf secreted it and opened it in his steadying hands. The glancing blow to his head must have concussed him slightly, but his healing was now kicking in. Behind him, he heard Stasia yelling at everyone to back off. That what could be done would be done.

Olaf needed this man to live and be able. People had seen the wound. They would know it should be fatal. He glanced around and saw Anatoly climbing down the cliff-face on the side of the dell. He was moving too fast for a normal human. If people in the crowd noticed, there could be hell to pay.

If Anatoly noticed what he was about to do there would also be hell to pay, but Olaf was not going to let Oskar die if he could help it. Hissing slightly as he sliced his palm with the scalpel, Olaf filled the nanite vial with his blood. Dropping the blade, he then placed his bleeding hand at the top of the wound, so the blood would seep down into it.

Waiting, with his hand holding Oskar on his side, Olaf felt the deep cut healing. His blood would be lost among Oskar's around the wound. Slowly, carefully, he lowered Oskar back to his side. He knew he was breaking the rules. He knew the nanites in his system were different—that they were guaranteed to change someone. Not a potentially lethal one like his mother had endured, but one slowly over time.

Lilith was Lilith. She had kept replication as a high priority in the nanite programming for Boris's line. So long as the host would survive, and a single nanite remained, it would replicate.

Olaf did not care for the consequences. Either people would accept Oskar when it happened, or Olaf would find him a place in New Romanovka.

It was better than having a man die because of him.

The gurgling gasps subsided to normal breathing. Olaf did not even notice that Anatoly was at his side. Having seen the bloody scalpel on the ground, he retrieved it and slowly placed it in a pocket to deal with later.

Olaf raised the vial of nanites to Oskar's mouth. Anatoly did not make any comment. Olaf had almost certainly put the cut hand in or over the wound. The damage was already done. All any more of Olaf's nanites would do now was speed the man's recovery.

Anatoly hoped on one hand that it had not been simple impulsiveness that had caused Olaf to act. On the other hand, losing even one person in this clusterfuck would be like lighting a fuse leading to a room full of gunpowder.

The group that had gathered around Andrev had drawn weapons on Stasia when her father had fallen. At the same time, a mass of firearms had been pointed at them from all around. A few, including Olaf and Stasia, had rushed to Oskar's aid. There was murder in the eyes of a half-dozen in the group that was still pointing weapons at those who had physically allied themselves with Andrev by proximity.

Olaf focused on getting the rest of the medical nanites, with his blood, into Oskar.

Anatoly started when he heard a worry-wracked voice ask grimly, "What is the prognosis?"

Olaf answered, "He will live. There may be," he paused, then continued, "complications. But I will explain them to him when he wakes."

He then rose to his feet and took off the long-sleeved t-shirt he had been wearing over his armor. He picked the bullets out of it and ground out, "Fifty-caliber armor piercing. I will have to give Lilith my compliments." Taking them in his hand, he turned to face the crowd.

Stalking across the field, he threw the bullets. He paused as he saw that Stasia's knife sheath was empty. Looking at the body for the first time, he saw the hilt in the eye. He grimaced and turned to Stasia.

"I'm sorry you had to do that. I'm also thankful you acted so quickly. If he'd shot again, I could be dead. Still, I'm sorry it was you who had to act," he said softly to her, gently laying a hand on her shoulder.

He had to respect her, but there was a trickle of fear in that respect. Here was a woman who was willing and able to act as she felt necessary. No matter what. First against the monster that her mother had become. Now against the madness she had seen in her father.

She shrugged and said angrily, loudly with bitterness shadowing her voice, "He looked too long into the darkness, and it consumed him. He was no longer a man I could call Father. That man had become lost beneath the curdled hate of war. He could see no end, nor did he want an end. Your offer gives us a chance to end all of this." Tears were streaming down her face.

She turned her gaze to the crowd and continued in a firm voice despite the tears. "I mourn the man he was when I was a child. I will not mourn the man I killed here today. That man was a rabid dog and a danger to everyone here. To those who supported him, drop your weapons and leave. Do not return to the war, I beg you. Go home. Find who you were."

She paused, then continued. "Those who want no part of ending the fight, go with them. Protect them as you see fit. Oskar lives. So, all I ask is do not take revenge out on those who supported my father's point of view." Her voice cracked with grief.

Still, she continued, "Those who do seek an end, I ask you to stay and hear us out. Hear this good man out. The man who was attacked by one of us, and instead of helping himself, he first sought to aid the one injured by an attack aimed for him."

Then she stumbled forth and crumpled, weeping over the corpse of the man who had once been her father. The man who had become something she had been forced to act against.

CHAPTER SIXTEEN

Olaf was incredibly annoyed. Traveling to the arranged rendezvous for gathering the clans, as Oskar had put it, was supposed to be straightforward. They were moving in four groups of twelve to sixteen.

Unfortunately, Olaf could smell the death-stench coming off the platoon headed straight for his group. At best, they were a group associated with a Vampire challenging Raina. That seemed very unlikely, and stopping them to ask wasn't an option.

Especially since they were in identical battledress and armor to what Raina's troops wore.

They were downwind far enough to give Olaf time to signal to his squad of eleven and Stasia to find ambush positions. He then saw a hollow to struggle out of his kit, especially his pants, as fast as possible. He only had one other pair left, and he did not want to be forced to wear them for however long it took relief to arrive.

He may well be the best marksman in the group, but that was beside the point right now. He was the fastest pursuer available. That would be needed. Not a single member of the patrol could be allowed to escape. Not within two hours travel from the rendezvous site.

Oskar had assured Olaf that the base was at least a day's travel from the rendezvous. It was still morning, so this had to be at least a two-day patrol, but more likely three or four days at the slow pace they were setting.

Once he was down to his armor, Olaf poked his head up and looked around. He swore as he glanced out of the hollow he had been stripping down in.

Their scouts were moving in close to where his squad had gone to ground.

Then a somewhat crazy idea crossed his mind. Looking for the locations he had last seen each squad member, he quickly calculated the optimum lines of fire down the hill. The enemy was advancing halfway up the slope. His people had gone to ground near the crest.

He started the change. If he could trick the advancing troops to shift their advance even five degrees downslope, he would give his own people a significant edge. One they would need while ambushing the thirty or more men in the patrol.

If he charged out as a bear and killed the two scouts, then lumbered off at the first gunshots in the right direction, he might be able to tempt the whole patrol into giving chase. It would allow him a personal assessment of the quality of the opposition. That sort of thing was always a bonus.

He crept closer to the cautiously approaching scouts. As a bear, his form would not instantly trigger the scouts to alert if spotted. At least not on the subconscious level. He was already close enough to reach them before they could do more than scream, but he didn't want to move at his full speed. He wanted it to look like they had disturbed a bear just out of hibernation. One that was in the mind frame to kill and eat anything.

He made it to within thirty meters before he charged. One of the scouts was looking straight at the undergrowth he was hidden in. With a bear's bellow, he burst from the underbrush. The men he was facing were expecting gunfire or a man. They froze for a few critical seconds. Almost everyone he knew, apart from Stasia, paused at the unexpected.

They were also making a mistake in how they scouted. They were moving too closely together. There was barely three feet separating them, and Olaf's charge bowled them both onto their backs. He mauled one across the neck, and the bright spray of blood told him his claws had ripped through the jugular.

Turning his head to the other scout, he bit down on the forearm that was scrabbling at the pistol holster on his belt. Olaf's jaws tore the muscle and shattered the bone.

The scout was a screamer, and Olaf thanked the gods for that. If he'd been a whimperer, the plan would be less likely to work.

Within a minute, he could hear a group of men, probably around twenty, rushing forward. They were not as well trained as they thought, or there was more than a platoon patrolling. From the sides, he could hear another five or six converging. Then he felt a line of fire cross his arse just before the crack of gunfire.

It hurt, but he kept concentration and lumbered off at the gunfire. The wound was more embarrassing than truly danger-ous. Once he hit the heavier undergrowth off the game trail, he moved at his faster speed. He traveled in a relatively straight line away from the shots for about five hundred feet and left the sign a normal bear in a hurry would.

Then he circled back when he hit an area with some stone to cover the change in direction. He moved carefully so as not to leave trail sign for about a minute. His wound was already heal-ing. Finally, he turned to approach the site where he had started the mayhem.

As he ambled back to the site, he thought about what that short time had shown him. Their marksmanship was better than he had counted on. Everything else in their training showed a lack of it. It was as if they were acting as twentieth century civilians thought soldiers acted, rather than how they should behave. His people had been paralleling the path. They were traveling along it.

And his people had still been moving faster and gave off fewer clues that they were there. That was why the partisan movement had survived and grown. They had been able to turn patrols away from critical areas.

Voices in an odd Belarussian and Russian mixed dialect cut into his thoughts, "... I ain't gonna let no bear take one of us out," he heard a surly voice say. Olaf paused then moved forward cautiously, one paw lifting at a time, his body low to the ground.

The voice continued, "I'm gonna take my squad and hunt it down. It left us a trail."

A voice with an edge of authority cut in and said, "Raina isn't going to like that, Gleb."

The first voice continued a little less trenchantly, "There ain't nothing in this Raina's gonna like, Zhenja. We just lost two men to wildlife. At least if we bring some bear back, we can prove it was wildlife, not the terrorists. Do you want one of her side-kicks coming on our next patrol with one of the monster things?"

There was silence, so Olaf froze. He was around two hundred meters away at this point.

The second voice quavered and answered, "Yeah, you're right. Take your men and half of Makar's squad. I'll put scouts back out, and we'll move out at half the regular pace. Catch up with us tonight. Once you get back to us, I'll radio in that we have the claws of the killer. Just make sure you cut 'em off. With Raina assembling a force to head east, I don't want to be singled out as less than competent. Her sending one of her bodyguards with us could be the least of our problems. We could be sent east as scouts for the force she's gathering."

"Yessir. I will. Her bodyguards creep me out. Anything to avoid having one of them leading us. As for being sent east? No, thanks." The original speaker finished with a shudder. Then he started organizing the men.

They had a radio. Olaf was swearing across three languages in his head. The partisans hadn't mentioned them having combat comms or radios. And now his rifle was on the other side of the enemy.

The only good news was that the enemy only had one radio from the sound of it. He was unsure of the combat comms. Those would be short ranged anyway, but he would have to shadow them and locate the radioman to take him down before a report could be sent.

It was not long before Olaf was forced to act. Fortunately, he had spotted the radioman before the first shot from the ambush group rang out. It was also fortunate that the half-dozen scouts were still closing in on the remaining ten soldiers in the ambush zone.

Olaf had been about to charge the radioman when the back of the radio splintered under fire. He froze as the scouts came beating feet towards their ambushed comrades.

Those scouts had done the stupid thing. Reacting instead of thinking. Three of them found themselves dead or dying before they were able to do any good. The others had gone to ground, taking cover on the lee side of the hill.

Unfortunately, so did the fifteen that had to move out to track the sign Olaf had left. They quickly headed for the sound of the guns. At least most of them did. Olaf could hear the surly lead order one of them back to base.

Olaf had his first target. If the patrol didn't radio in, another patrol might be sent. If that man reached the base, another patrol would be sent. Probably a larger one. If not larger, then one led by a Vampire and containing some 'controlled' Nosferatu.

That man had to die. Olaf turned, picking up the sound of a man crashing through the spring forest away from the cracks of gunfire. He did not attempt to be quiet. After all, there wasn't a human alive that could outrun a normal bear, let alone Olaf. He had failed to follow the age-old wisdom—to have someone next to him that he was faster than.

Olaf reached his target before he had traveled even half a kilometer away from the gunfire. The man desperately tried to dodge the bear charging after him. Olaf simply stretched out a paw after he passed the man to send him tumbling.

There was a sickening crack of bones as the runner tumbled awkwardly to the ground. Even from behind, where he had slowed, Olaf could see that the man was not breathing. His neck was at an unnatural angle, having snapped in the tumble.

Olaf headed back towards the firefight. The enemy seemed to be pouring suppressive fire uphill. Perhaps they considered themselves dead already. Their ambushers would have better shots than they could hope to achieve from below, but they were not even trying to disengage.

They were stubborn beyond the point of the sensible. Any of Boris's troops in a similar situation would be trying to disengage as a body. More to the point, none of Boris's force would have gone off mission to hunt a bear!

Stalking the sounds of gunfire through the undergrowth, Olaf found himself acting as executioner. He zeroed in on where the bursts of fire were coming from and crept behind the target. Often, following the stink of shit and urine was enough. They were so fixated forward on the single shots coming from Stasia's force, all he had to do was make a small effort to be quiet.

Then he was atop them. With a single swipe of his paw, he either snapped their neck or severed the jugular. That sped them on to whatever afterlife they belonged to.

They had either been caught by complete surprise or did not know enough to empty themselves of waste before a battle. Either was possible, although Olaf hoped it was the latter. That would be another point against their professionalism.

By the time he stalked toward the last half-dozen or so of the enemy patrol, they seemed to notice something was creeping along the firing line they had formed. Almost as one, they rose to run—making themselves perfect targets for Stasia and the other ambushers.

They were cut down in a volley of fire before they had gone ten feet.

Olaf stilled, listening for movement, for someone in the enemy patrol he had missed. He heard a few groans from the injured on the road, but not even a whisper of breath from the nearby woods.

The guerrillas kept cover and stayed silent. Good discipline there.

Olaf let out a roar before he lumbered onto the road. No one fired at him, despite the sight he must have been. The front of his body was covered in blood, to the point it was still dripping from his fur now and then.

Once he reached the path, he turned and lumbered towards the dell where he had stripped off his gear. Changing to human form, he was upset that blood and gore transferred between his forms. He would need to wash in a stream or river to get clean. Someone else would need to carry his equipment, or at least pack his clothes and armor so he could. That would be uncomfortable.

He heard Stasia coming through the bush in a rage. She was furious with him about something, he was sure. Probably the risks he had taken.

"Do you even have a mind?" she thundered at him, "or do you put it to the side whenever it pleases you? You are supposed to be leading the force once it is gathered. You can't do that if you're dead!"

Olaf was standing there just in his pants. She glared at him when she noticed that his armor was on the ground. "And you didn't even wear your armor!"

He looked at her and said, "Of course not! I was trying to make them think it had been a local, normal, bear. Bears don't walk around in armor. Their reactions, and that of your own people, told me a lot." He stared down at her, meeting her glare.

When she stayed silent, he continued. "Your people are disciplined. I think you could have taken her base if it weren't for the fact she has several subservient Vampires and a group of Nosferatu she had controlled. And, of course, the energy weapon they have. With the right equipment or planning, even that tank should not have been an insurmountable obstacle to defeating her."

He was still very concerned about the energy weapon. No one had any idea of the size it was, nor of the range and accuracy it might have.

Stasia was grim when she said, "And what if they had had it with the patrol?"

Olaf rolled his eyes at her. There was no way that a group had managed to mass produce something like that after the Fall.

If a group had managed to before the Fall, then they would currently rule the world.

Stasia slapped his arse, hard. On the side where he had been shot. He hissed in pain as she struck the still healing, tender section. She stared daggers at him and said, "You *did* get shot. I thought so. No more risks."

Wincing slightly, he responded, "I can't agree to that. I need to take risks in the assault. I am the best chance of gaining a quick breakthrough and the best suited to taking out a Vampire or three. The other Weres can deal with Nosferatu, but I would only give Vassily credit for being a probable equal to any Vampire we encounter. That means both of us will need to lead from the front."

She glared at him, then nodded. Before he could react, she pulled him down into a kiss. She blushed furiously, then turned away whispering, "Just try to stay alive. For me."

He whispered back, "I will," though he was not sure she heard his reply.

CHAPTER SEVENTEEN

Boris was happy with how everything was going. As comfortable as he could be instituting a siege against Viktor and the tactics he had chosen. It was like fighting a war in the seventeenth century.

Viktor had chosen to pack central St. Petersburg with civilians as well as his troops. Boris could besiege it, and within a month he would be walking through the town with minimal casualties on his own side. Five hundred years ago, that was what he would have done.

It would have been the standard practice for the day and age. At the time, soldiers, himself included, didn't consider an assault worth the risk when a siege would do the job. Why take thousands of casualties assaulting a fortified position when you could starve them out?

Now, he saw civilians as a valuable resource, especially since the Fall. Every person was an asset.

He was going to have to assault at some point in the next two weeks. Before food supplies became a critical problem inside.

Besides, he was not the Cossack, with the brutally simple philosophy they held to, anymore. He couldn't see those effectively being held hostage in the city as worth less than his men.

Then, there was also the fact he could assault fortified skyscrapers from the top down with his shuttles.

The siege lines were dug, and he should have had three regiments preparing to assault. Unfortunately, the Estonians were not there yet.

He had a screen of patrols to the south. Janna was on her way with a battalion of mixed militia units. Her last message to him had concerned the Estonians. She was worried. They had been through some political upheaval since the treaty signing.

She was coming with more than the agreed upon company of reinforcements because of it. Boris could tell it had her worried. If she was concerned about potential problems from the leadership, so was he.

His response was to put platoon-sized patrols out on the southern flank. They were to approach cautiously, and retreat at speed if there was any suspicious behavior from the Estonian force.

That had been three days ago. He needed at least a week to fully prep any force for the assault. The three shuttles were continually rotating platoons through for training in assault landings from them. Everyone not training was on alert. In four days, they would have to switch to briefings on assaulting down a skyscraper.

In six days, the engineers would have finished the two-story wooden skyscraper mock-up. They would have to start cycling a company at a time through then. Boris noted the need to complete the training rotation.

Then he smelled a Were in wolf form in the camp.

There were only so many reasons one would take that shape inside the camp. Checking his watch, he confirmed that training against Weres was not the reason. That was still hours away.

That meant that either the siegeworks were being assaulted, or the Estonians had fired on one of his patrols. Boris devoutly hoped it was the former, but somehow knew it was the latter.

With the differences in equipment, there was no chance the latter had been a mistake. Viktor's forces still used ceramic plate insert armor, and even at a distance that was distinctive from that used by Boris's forces.

He waited while the Were shifted to human form. Once the Were was human again, Boris stated, "Report."

"Estonian forces have been encountered, sir. They did not wait for sight confirmation range. The first shot was fired at over eight hundred meters. One casualty as we exited range. Fifty caliber sniper round."

Boris looked up and cursed. Even his forces armor was not proof against fifty caliber, armor-piercing rounds. "Casualty status?"

"Being evacuated on a stretcher. He will live, sir," a bitter tone came into the professional tone the soldier had been using so far, "but without a leg for the time being."

"Better one man than a company or battalion being hit from behind by people they think are allies, private," Boris answered sternly.

"Yessir. I'm simply angry at the betrayal. Not at the methods used to discover the treachery," the soldier answered firmly. Boris simply nodded. Anger at a buddy being injured or killed was normal.

Boris scribbled movement orders to his two designated ready regiments. It would weaken his siege lines to a reserve of a battalion a sector, but the risk of an attack from hostile forces outside those lines was something that had to be dealt with.

Forces facing away from an incoming attack would always be at a severe disadvantage.

"Get these to Colonels Vilosty and Terrance. We move out within the hour. I will organize the artillery we need."

The soldier took the paperwork, nodded, and left the tent.

Boris rose from behind his camp desk. Exiting the tent, he barked an order to several of the runners. While he had combat comms available, he restricted their use to active assault operations.

<<<>>>

"We simply cannot get them out of their dugouts that fast, sir," one of the Artillery officers was telling Boris about the expected movement time on three batteries of horse guns. "We have them dug in. You said fixed positions, so they are in tightly fixed positions. We didn't put ramp space at the back of their positions. We traded that for better overhead cover."

Boris responded, "So, you threw out the book here in horse artillery, is that what you are telling me? I have the mortars pulling as we speak. The two howitzers are being pulled from their positions now. But horse guns cannot move in time to be dug in when we confront the enemy? An enemy that is using anti-material rifles for sniping?" The officer blanched at the chill in Boris's tone.

The fifty-caliber round was unlikely to destroy, or even damage, a well dug in horse gun. In large part, that was due to camouflage. The rifled horse cannon with anti-personnel rounds were intimidating.

Boris said, "If that's the case, fine. If they get on the road within the next forty minutes, you'll keep your rank. If not, then you are demoted, Major. We build ramps into our fixed gun positions for a reason—in case everything goes to hell."

Boris turned and left the position. He was so angry he didn't notice a senior lieutenant following him for the first half-minute or so. In fact, he didn't see it until one of his guards cleared his throat. Whirling, he turned his glare on the man.

The lieutenant said, "Sir, there is one battery that can be pulled. Mine. All three guns have jury-rigged, wooden drop ramps. My sergeant said that the guns have to be movable from a position."

"And why didn't you bring this up during the meeting?" Boris asked.

"Because the Major ordered me to destroy them, and I did not, sir," the lieutenant said nervously. "If your sergeant tells you something, then it is necessary."

Boris grunted, and nodded. Many junior officers felt that way. Often, but not always, they were right. In this case, Boris needed to know more. "Still, you couldn't tell me this earlier?"

The junior officer swallowed hard, then shook his head no. Swallowing, he said, "The Major is vindictive, sir. My men would be last to be dug in in the future. And… I was afraid. But I also don't want the infantry to suffer from a lack of guns."

Boris looked at the man. Solid, but not bright. He paused and recalled his record. Barely scraped into officer training and had a knack with horses. The main reason he was in Artillery was he knew how to take care of horses. He left maintaining the guns to their crews, but kept a close eye on logistics. He also made sure his unit had spare wheels for the carriages and paid himself to have the horses re-shod more often than the quartermasters agreed to cover. Fastest travel rate for any gun unit.

He might not be the brightest officer, but he was perfect for his rank in the Artillery. He may even make a good captain. Above all else, he was competent for his position. Even better, his guns would get where they were needed faster than anyone else.

"Corporal Korhonen, go with this lieutenant and make sure no one troubles him as he pulls his guns. Sergeant Syomin, strip the major's rank, send him to the trenches. Tell the captains if one of them gets a battery of guns out as fast at that young man, he will be given a field promotion to major. And make it clear I want those ramps dug before I get back."

Boris's mind raced as he thought about his planned ambush site. The guns could be dug into cut sites at the top of the over-looking hills. The valley was the only real choke point left on the Estonian's approach. There was no way to move the logistics of a regiment through any other position within a day's travel to the South.

Boris sighed. Having only one guaranteed battery would complicate things. No matter how careful a leader was, there was always someone who rose above their level of competence. Boris hoped he did not have any more in positions that became critical.

CHAPTER EIGHTEEN

Boris and his lead battalions arrived at the choke point not more than three hours before the Estonians could be expected to arrive. After putting out four company-sized patrols into the woods on either side of the planned ambush site, Boris had the rest start digging foxholes, both for themselves and their patrolling comrades.

One of the shuttles landed carefully behind a hill, out of sight from any approaching enemies. Boris didn't want to kill the Estonians. They were treacherous bastards, but he needed to know why.

As other elements arrived, he positioned them. Two howitzers behind the right-side hill, the other on the left. Three mortars behind each. Troops in foxholes on the crest and base of both. Cannon positions were being dug into each ridgeline by the infantry.

He still didn't know if he was going to have three or six field guns

The foxholes at the base of the hill were re-covered with turf. He wanted whatever scouts the enemy had deployed to be captured or annihilated behind the hills, where the road curved to head straight north.

He was disappointed in the preparations he had made against their scouts. There were no scouts unless the Estonians had a more substantial body of troops then any of his reports suggested was possible. A full regiment was rarely used as scouts. When there was only a reinforced regiment at most that the Estonians could have spared, this had to be the primary force. The Latvians would probably risk a raid if the Estonians stripped their southern border.

Boris headed back to the shuttle. It was on standby, waiting for the signal from the firing howitzers that they were boxed in. His scouting companies were to take positions to cut off any retreat. While he waited, he was informed the second battery of cannons had arrived.

He was waiting more than an hour from first spotting the first column before the howitzers fired. That would mean the central column was in the pocket.

The shuttle jumped into the air at the signal. Boris had the radio set to external speaker.

"You are surrounded and outgunned. I will offer you a chance to lay down your arms and surrender." Before he could even finish, shots were fired at the shuttle from the force below. His cannon on the hilltops responded with a volley.

Wherever a shell struck, a platoon of the enemy was taken from the calculation of forces. The shrapnel scythed through troops, killing and maiming. Perhaps an average of fifteen men became instant casualties in the ragged, too-tight, marching formation.

Blackened ground centered where each shell had exploded. Surrounding that was the mangled dead. No unit could absorb a casualty rate of fifty percent in seconds and still be combat effective. As he watched, the formation shifted.

Men spread out and hit the ground. The roadway was

suddenly empty as they searched for whatever cover or concealment they could find in the vacant space around it. Even a tuft of
grass was more than they had, standing on the roadway. Boris
could feel nothing but contempt for their training.

They should have moved to the roadside and spread out as
soon as the howitzer shells exploded behind them.

Boris could see officers running among their troops below
and the firing slowly ceased. He waited until no shots could be
heard, then continued, "We have you surrounded. Our forces
have cut your line of retreat. We control the air. You have two
options. Surrender or be slaughtered where you stand. Considering you attacked my forces despite a treaty yesterday, I suggest
you not test my patience."

The units that had been near where the cannon shells landed
were laying down their arms and walking clear of the rest of the
force with their arms raised. They knew they were defeated.
Slowly, more and more of the Estonian troops did the same.

Once the entire unit was more than a hundred meters away
from the weapons, a company was sent in to secure the few holdouts. As men stood from their foxholes on the ridges, Boris could
imagine the expressions on the faces of those holdouts.

Securing the willing surrenders took longer. First, a battalion
swept the area where the weapons had been dropped. Once they
were secure, two companies went through and patted down each
soldier, retrieving their ammunition and knives. Finally, they
were sent in company groups to near the logistics base he had
built up.

The best solution would be to simply send them home. In
good conscience, Boris could not risk it. It would be a two-week
turnaround for them to re-arm and be sent back. The timing of
their return would be just after he assaulted the towers, at most
six days later.

Even re-armed and returned, after a recent surrender they
would be slaughtered by his forces. Their morale was crushed. It

took months or even years for a unit to recover from being forced into a position in which they had to surrender.

But whoever was in charge in Estonia right now was an idiot.

Finally, Boris landed the shuttle to take on board the senior officers. He recognized none of them–they just did not match any descriptions of Estonia's senior officers that Janna had on file.

Boris started his interrogation with, "Why did the coup happen?"

The officers looked at each other uncomfortably, then the colonel sighed and answered in heavily accented Russian, "I am Colonel Rasmus Laar. The coup happened after a significant portion of the military families in the North had their families captured in a series of raids from Viktor. The government had assumed it would take him time to solidify his control after his father died. They sent us to capture a mine from Latvia. The whole operation was a disaster. We did not capture the mine due to the government diverting some of the supplies they had promised us. Many soldiers lost their families because of the government's assumptions."

"You signed the treaty *after* the coup. Why not stand by it?"

"What treaty? We were told the talks failed. Even had they succeeded, Viktor still has most of the families. We have letters in their handwriting. He threatened their lives if we did not do as he said," Colonel Laar said stoically. "They were our people. We could not simply leave them to be abused by Viktor. He is an animal with his people. Would you simply have ignored his demands?"

Boris snorted contemptuously and answered, "But every action you made risked those people more. If I had known about Viktor's actions sooner, I could have prepared sooner. I could have helped you. But instead, you decided to follow his demands."

He then paused as the 'What treaty?' comment sank in.

After a moment, he answered with obvious confusion, "Your ambassador signed the treaty. One Marakov, I believe."

The shuttle was so silent as he stopped, the footsteps of an ant would have sounded like those of an elephant. Slowly, as that sunk in, the faces of the officers switched from horrified to furious.

Laar exploded. "That *abordijaanus*. That *sittur*. He set us up! *He* is responsible for this!"

Boris thought that calling him the leftovers from an abortion was, perhaps, taking it a bit far. Saying he stank of farts was a fair comment.

Then the other officers were also furious at this revelation. There was a simmering anger in the air. Boris gave them some time to calm down. He was not immune to fury at such a deception.

"I still have to take you in as prisoners. My men simply will not trust you after the incident with a patrol," Boris stated as calmly as he could. He raised a hand to forestall any objections, continuing, "Nor would your men be fit for any such. Not for weeks, if not months. They were forced into an untenable position. Forced to surrender. Such things erode the will to fight and morale of a unit."

He paused, waiting for an objection. When there was none, he continued. "But we will keep you under guard. That presents the least risk to your families. If we treat you as enemy combatants, then Viktor will have to assume the same. I will not guarantee that we will recover them all. We will do everything we can to avoid their deaths. As we will for all civilians trapped in the city."

They looked at each other, then looked back at Boris. Colonel Laar took a grim tone when he answered, "That is all we can ask. Thank you for those efforts. I know it will cost your men."

"There is one more thing I can ask of you, however. Do you have any intelligence on Viktor? The more I know, the better. I knew his grandfather well. He was a hard man, but a competent officer and administrator. I can't see how he has a grandson, who seems bent on destroying that legacy. I only knew Viktor's father a little. He was determined to keep the region his father had left him intact. The only reason he pushed control south was to stamp out the rampant banditry."

The officers looked at one of the captains. His nametag said Turnig. Boris raised an interrogative eyebrow, and the man sighed.

"Yes, I know him personally," Turnig's voice took a quiver as he started to explain "In fact, I was raised alongside him. Same classes, many of the same training exercises in our youth. Until he was about ten, he was a nice enough kid, too. I wouldn't say he had a generous soul, but he understood the value of teamwork. Then his mother died. Things change dramatically in his household after that.

"His father was a hard man, but he had a blind spot for Viktor. Anyone who was gaining higher classroom ranks than him started to be transferred. Then some of us started getting beaten. I know, as I was one of those beaten.

"I think it twisted his view of what the world was. His father removed obstacles to him being ranked first as long as he worked hard. After the fourth time I was beaten, my family fled. I may not have survived a fifth. I was better at maths than him. God, I even tutored him for hours after the first beating. It still wasn't enough. He was better than me in some areas, but my trigonometry and geometry scores were always higher than his.

"I think he started to view talent as a myth. He is a competent leader himself, but he doesn't have the spark to make a great leader. That something extra that doesn't rely on knowledge alone. He is also convinced that no consequences ever apply to him. After all, if he achieved first in class, no one was beaten. But if someone else beat him, they were physically beaten, not him. There is an arrogance about him to those outside of his immediate group of sycophants. Them, he treats well. He even treats his soldiers fairly well. But the civilians of his lands have been suffering his ever-increasing tax system for years."

Boris thought about it for a while. His opponent had been almost trained to accept success as inevitable. Beyond that, he was arrogant. There were ways he could exploit that. The roof landings on occupied skyscrapers were a start. He was the only person in the region who could carry such landings out. Viktor would almost certainly not have thought of them.

He would have to wait and see how Viktor reacted. How this arrogance manifested.

A wave of relief washed over Boris as he heard how Viktor had been raised. While he had been overprotective with Olaf in many ways, everything Olaf had achieved was despite that. Boris's son could be far worse as a consequence of being protected. Perhaps it was more a matter of how Olaf had been protected compared to Viktor.

Boris had protected his son by restrictions rather than by making him feel he was the best at everything. Perhaps he had harmed Olaf, he realized now. But he had not disconnected him from those around him. Had always made him feel equal, but only equal, to those around him.

He was left with the gloomy thought of what damage his method of raising his eldest son had done.

CHAPTER NINETEEN

Olaf was tossing and turning. He was supposed to be asleep. He needed the rest if he was going to be in top form for tomorrow. He was the single Were going to the observation point, a spot the local partisans had found that was not patrolled or watched, yet overlooked the cave Raina based from.

He was worried his presence would give everything away. He could smell the wolf on all the Werewolves around him. They claimed that there was only the faintest bear scent about him, and then only when he was close.

Something niggled at his memory, though. He wished he could talk to Lilith about it. The less sleep he was getting, the more he wished it. Suddenly, it was like there was a burst of static in his head.

He writhed in pain. He was glad he had moved his sleeping place downstream of most of the others. His thrashing would have woken them, too.

Then the static broke, and a voice he recognized came through. <<*Olaf? Is that you?*>>

Remembering how cranky she got when he spoke to her verbally in the cave, he answered in his head. *"Lilith? How is this even possible? I thought I needed an implanted etheric transmitter to talk to you like this!"*

<<*Err... congratulations? You now have one.*>> Olaf felt an icy trickle through his brain. Through his entire body. << *Yup, your nanites reacted by finding the simplest way to end your emotional discomfort. It was starting to damage you physically. You need to stress less.*>>

Olaf mentally snorted. *"I'm stuck out on a limb with a fragile alliance of my forces and local partisans against at least three Vampires, an unknown number of Nosferatu, hundreds of humans soldiers, and a tank. I have a single medium railgun, two hundred rounds for it, and rifles, pistols, and shotguns with a small handful of grenades for the rest. Call it an assault force of around two hundred and fifty, although that number is rising. Small groups of partisans are trickling into rendezvous points every couple of hours."*

<<*See? Nothing to worry too much about. Nosferatu aren't even really a threat to you. One bite and your nanites will conflict with theirs.*>>

"First, that's not what I was worried about right then. I was more concerned about my scent giving away that a Were was in the area to an old Vampire like Raina. I must scout her position before I assault it!"

<<*Well, wash then. Wash the armor if it has been worn while you shifted. It is not like I left one of my creations with such an accidental flaw. Other Weres cannot smell you, then. A Vampire can't detect what a Were can't. Not unless they are of Bethany Anne's line, and all of them left.*>>

"But they still react to me. Why do they react?"

Sighing, Lilith answered, <<*You emit a low etheric signature. All the changed do. Nothing that can be tracked, but enough to subconsciously give an idea of who is more or less powerful when in each other's presence. I taught you that when you were a kid. You should know this.*>>

Olaf frowned as he went over his memories. He could not

remember being taught that. There was nothing there about relative strength and how it was detected.

<<*Just take a bath, and get some sleep. I'll adjust your levels temporarily, so you only need an hour or two. Just don't tell your father about the last bit. He can be touchy when I 'meddle' as he puts it. Do you want to send him a message? He has a communicator on his person.*>>

Olaf thought about it for a minute or two, then decided, "*No. Maybe after I scout. If he asks about me, you can tell him what happened.*"

Olaf got up and went to the stream, grabbing his armor on the way to wash it at the same time. It might dry before they left to scout. While Olaf was cleaning, Lilith kept nattering to him.

Finally, she reached the point. <<*So, why did you reach out to me, not your mother or father?*>>

Olaf thought about it for several minutes, then answered, "*You were the most likely to give me a straight answer without telling me off. I know I'm taking a few risks here, but the lead Vampire, Raina, is a monster. She's turning people into Nosferatu, then setting them loose on their families.*"

<< *Was my theory correct?*>> Lilith asked with a sudden intensity, <<*Do they seek their family by preference, or does drinking familial blood push them to a more controlled state?*>>

Olaf grimaced. He was glad as hell Stasia was not listening to this.

"*No evidence either way. I will see how they are in battle.*"

<< *Be careful of the Vampires. They have better functioning nanites than the Nosferatu. Your blood will not have the same effect on them,*>> Lilith cautioned before the link went dead. There was a short static in his head then silence.

'*Just like Lilith,*' he thought grumpily to himself '*Gets the information she wants, then drops the line.*'

It had been nice to talk to someone from home.

He still had a mission in the morning. After drying himself as best he could, he went back to the sleeping bag. To his surprise, he found himself suddenly awake, feeling more rested than he had since the shuttle crash, as the steel grey of pre-dawn hit the horizon.

He could get used to needing so little sleep.

<<<>>>

The group of local partisans and leaders scouting the enemy base left before dawn. Olaf was a little nervous as they crossed a beaten patrol path, despite repeated assurances that a patrol had passed the area yesterday. Apparently, Raina's patrols stuck to a regular schedule, even if patrols were attacked.

They were more than forty kilometers from the ambush anyways. Any extra patrols shouldn't be here. The pattern the partisans followed previously was to strike and flee. To patrol closer would be pointless unless they had received word something was up. Half the group leaders were going with Olaf on this recon patrol. More had wanted to, but Olaf had very quickly put the brakes on that.

"We may be intercepted," he started, then raised a hand to forestall any objections, "Even if we are not, some need to stay behind to keep on top of everyone. Keep the watch-posts manned, and the noise of the camp to a minimum. We are the largest group of partisans to form this close to Raina's camp. Everyone needs to be reminded of that. With no leadership present, mistakes could lead to the discovery of the force."

To his surprise, Stasia agreed with him. She felt that at least two-thirds of the leadership had to stay behind. Leading by example, she volunteered to stay back.

Olaf focused on the present. The local guide indicated they were reaching the overlook point. Even from five hundred meters away, he could hear sounds of a significant movement being prepared. Far larger than the loss of that single patrol would account for. Once they reached the site, he took cover and concealment. Looking down, he could see units forming up around the tank.

The tank looked fearsome. It was a heavily modified T-72 main battle tank. Although outdated at the Fall, it was still a viable weapon system. More so now, with the general lack of artillery. It would be a monster on a battlefield with nothing to challenge it. Only the railguns on the New Romanovkan shuttles would stand a chance against it.

Olaf brought a pair of old-fashioned field glasses to his face. Looking through them, he could get a better count on the number of troops forming up around the tank. More than two hundred and fifty.

It was slightly less than he had been expecting. Then again, there was the patrol that had been eliminated. That could account for the extra troops he had been expecting to leave once his relief force was spotted.

The partisans were operating in terrain that only a madman or madwoman would send troops into. Operating in heavily forested mountains and hills was a good way to get the main battle tank bogged down and left exposed.

That tank left Olaf with a hard decision to make. The railgun he had was salvaged—it was not a standard weapon carried by Boris's forces. While the artillery and mortars his original force would have could disable that monster, nothing in the force he had left behind could destroy it.

That left him with a dilemma. No matter the size of the force he managed to gather to assault this base, they would take casualties. Even if they managed to infiltrate close, the cave system that troops were rushing equipment out of to the force that was leaving would make that the case. The railgun would reduce their casualties on that assault.

Then he saw the main gun on the tank. That was no standard main gun. Red discharges arced along its barrel. The square shape of the barrel, everything about it, told Olaf that this was the weapon that had taken out his shuttle. That meant it probably had the same effective range as a Railgun. Line of sight.

Any force caught in the open by such a weapon would be massacred. There was no question about it. It would be able to fire before any shuttle could target it. And, while removing the railguns from a shuttle was relatively easy, his father may need all of them for the assault on St. Petersburg.

Removing them was easy. Putting them back on the shuttle was not. New Romanovka simply did not have the industrial setup all the way there yet. The new craft that had been designed were pure troop transports. They weren't ready to be produced yet. But seating the railguns required a precision of machining that was destroyed when they were taken off. Olaf had only done it from his shuttle because it was a write-off.

Olaf swore. If that damned tank had been armed with a standard main gun, then there would have been no problem. Now, he was going to have to send his railgun team around the edge. He would have to make it five of his precious Weres. That was the only way to allow such a group to avoid any possible interception by enemy troops.

An additional concern was that the tank was obviously running on full electric motors. Had someone in the base cracked etheric generation? And how had they overcome the limitations that had prevented Boris from converting his tanks to the same? A large enough etheric generator to power a tank created a bubble around it that made any armament on them useless without turning the generator off. They were too small for the gunport methodology Bethany Anne's team had made work.

Then again, the weapon that had struck the shuttle had simply ripped through the shuttle's bubble. Perhaps a gunport was irrelevant. Or perhaps it was powered by a method that no-one else had thought of.

They would have to circle the base patrol perimeter, losing as much as a day's start on the force they were to follow. Weres should be able to make up a day over the week Olaf estimated should be between Major Petrova. It would have taken four or five days to organize a full movement of forces from a cold start.

Before he left to scout energy sources, they had assumed they would have time to plan any assault. The focus had been digging in the Fall-back position. Military forces able to switch operational footings suddenly was a myth.

Olaf switched his focus from the departing force to the base layout. There were two layers of razor wire. That was easy enough to circumvent with good troops. His twenty-five would split to cover that. Snipers up there could help, taking out the two dug-in machine gunners closest and covering the cave mouth. But three of the pits would not be able to be sniped from there. The range was too far.

He swore, and guilt flowed into him. There looked to be around a hundred men staying behind. His force numbered around three hundred. Without the sloppy patrols and the possibility to infiltrate snipers, any assault he could make would be suicide. As it was, without the railgun it would still be costly.

Grenades were rare among the partisans. They had an average of one each to the four standard grenades, two smoke, and one thermite grenade his men carried. Guilt welled up in him as he quickly estimated the casualty difference he would be asking of the partisans. Forty to fifty more casualties. At least ten deaths. But he had to weigh that up against the two hundred or more outright deaths the tank would cause if there wasn't a weapon available to Major Petrova to take out the tank.

Before they left the observation site, Olaf confirmed the tank was headed towards the highway. It was a logical choice. Travel along the edges of a road or the road itself would be the fastest way east. The local partisans had told him the largest beaten path out of the base met the highway.

He could only hope that his logic proved right.

<<<>>>

There was shouting as he put forth his plan. Several of the Partisan leaders were furious that Olaf was proposing to send away the railgun and a team.

Vassily was furious that they considered their own troop's lives more valuable than Olaf's troops. Petrova would be fighting the tank on low hills and plains—ground guaranteed to give the weapon greater range. Even if the base had smaller versions of that terrifying weapon, they would have better cover against it. If the assault failed, the mountainous terrain behind the base would allow them to fall back with minimal additional casualties.

Petrova's force would have to dig in. Falling back from whatever cover they could dig would be suicide. They would be lucky to escape with fifty percent losses. Considering that they would be infantry in the open, those losses would almost certainly be dead to that hell weapon.

Their attack would be safer since Olaf had spotted the communications post during the scouting mission. He volunteered to personally move in with the first wave to take it out. Behind the three bunkers, it was still more exposed than Boris or any of his commanders would have left it. A concrete bunker, there were enough explosives amongst the supplies scavenged from the shuttle to guarantee it would be taken out quickly.

It had been his volunteering to take the riskiest role in the assault that had turned the tide in the argument. Junior leaders respected it, saw their seniors as asking for him to betray his forces in their favor. They could respect someone who was willing to take personal risks that might make up the difference.

If it was set with a crush fuse, he could deliver the demo pack in bear form. In that form, he was confident this enemy would not be able to successfully target him. Throw it into the communications bunker then run like hell for the cave.

His platoon had objected. Heavily. The assault was planned

for four days from now. They had more partisans than they could have hoped for. Surely, Olaf could take a less risky role, they thought. Only Vassily had not raised any objections.

When asked, he answered, "He's the best man, with the best Wereform, for the job. Besides, as a bear, he's *fast*. The job needs that more than anything."

The large number of partisans had forced them to move farther away from the base, leaving a small team to keep an eye out for any changes on the base. Ten men, picked by Oskar and Stasia, with a single member of the small local partisan band. Their knowledge of the area around the enemy headquarters was critical to any success.

They were being treated like pearls without price in two ways. They were being put with assault teams and reserves. But to protect against any possible filth in their hearts, everyone was watching them carefully. None of them were allowed to even go to the latrine alone.

Other partisans had enforced that, not Olaf. That anyone could survive this close to the enemy base made them the highest risk for any breach of operational security. In Olaf's opinion, the local group had taken the suspicion with a resigned but stoic acceptance. This was the best chance to remove the terror that had encompassed their lives for so long.

Supply was a problem. Many of the partisans came in with only a day or two of food. What was left from the shuttle reserve packs had been distributed, but with a ban on active hunting—lest the gunfire be heard—they were relying on snares to make a difference. Most of the partisan groups had bases, but in the field survived on whatever could be scrounged.

Some of the local edible roots were dug up. Snares were laid. Everyone knew they needed to take that base. Those who retreated east would only survive the week if the relief force defeated the enemy and continued forward.

The first two days would be Olaf briefing them on how to

take on the Nosferatu they would almost certainly encounter. His remaining Weres were tasked with taking on the two known male Vampires. Raina was his, so long as he was still standing. If he fell, the plan was to fall back to the east. To link up with Major Petrova. The pilot, Vlad, was with the eastern reserve to make sure the partisans would be identified as friendlies. Pilots had a distinctive scent from their nanite package. Weres among the relief force would recognize it.

One of the concerns was that the Vampires might be able to act in the daylight. They would have to be on the lookout. No partisan had seen them and lived. The plan was based on the possibility that they were able to act during the day somehow. Possibly armored or with special clothing.

The plan was solid. While it was a risk of defeat in detail, that was countered by dispersal of Raina's forces. The number of men manning the bunkers had been confirmed to have reduced since the tank, and its infantry supports had been sent.

Her base was operating on a skeleton crew. The only disappointment Olaf felt over the whole situation was that both her confirmed Vampire supporters were present. She had to trust the leader of the tank force.

He had feared one would have been sent to look for the missing patrol.

His hope for one being sent with the tank force had also been unfulfilled. In the scheme of things, that made it an even break.

But perhaps the leader of the tank force was a Vampire. No-one had entered or left the tank while they watched. The smell, her stench, was so strong he could not even smell the other Vampires he had been told of.

Stasia had been a great help in gathering the support for his plan. There was a mixture of being well known and respected in the community and outright fear of crossing her, especially after how her father had died, that allowed her leverage.

One of her brothers had refused to combine his band with the assault, instead of retreating to the West. The other saw what their father had done as a breach of everything he had taught his children. While grieving over the necessity of his father's death, he blamed that man, and not his sister.

Junior leaders had taken over after senior leaders hesitated. Most of the rank and file partisans were on board. Some of the top leaders seemed to want the interminable warfare to continue. Olaf even understood why.

With the never-ending conflict, they saw their leadership as never in doubt. Without it, those leaders could lose status and control. They had been fighting for so long they knew little else in life.

They would need help from the outside to survive and prosper after the conflict ended. The only logical source of it was through Olaf, from Boris's lands.

Others were highly supportive because they were so tired of the fighting. The partisans were a distilled group of fighters. Although they were less disciplined than he was used to, they still had some of the attributes of military discipline and loyalty.

Their training, those that had survived, made up the difference. Rather than the formal training of Boris's forces, every day was training. Survival, for them, had been all the training Olaf could have asked of anyone.

Those who had actively objected to the plan were being prepped to be sent away, to the North, under the guard of those who would make up the northern reserve and assault force.

Watches from his people had been synchronized. All six parts of his assault force had at least two.

Now that enough people in the leadership was on board with the plan, he communicated with Lilith again. *"Can you link me through to the command of the relief force, please, Lil?"*

Olaf could almost feel the shy smile in her response. The implanted transceiver allowed much more than simple communication. Emotions and underlying images flowed through the link as well. *<<Connecting you through now.>>*

A familiar, but unexpected, voice answered. *"Olaf, why the fuck have you been silent? You should have called in when you crashed! Your dad was a mess, and I had to volunteer to take command down here to stop him from coming. That would have been a disaster!"* It took Olaf a moment for the voice to register as Paul's.

<<You are being unfair, Paul,>> Lilith scolded over the link, *<<His original device was destroyed. Stress caused his nanites to spontaneously create an implanted transmitter>>*

"What. The. Fuck. Boris is not going to be happy about that," Paul said, then he paused and took a deep breath. Olaf could almost see Paul making a scrunching movement then a throwaway gesture with his hands.

After he took another deep breath, he continued. "Situation report."

Olaf summarized the information his scouting of the base, the plan of attack and the rough layout of the base, as well as the numbers of the force that seemed to be moving in the direction of the relief force. He concluded with, "Even with the loss of a patrol, none of the partisans have detected a significant change in their operations. They sent a reinforced patrol to investigate the lost patrol, but that seems to be their SOP."

Paul sounded concerned when he said, "But you plan to assault this base while low on rations. With troops of unknown training or psychological state."

"Anatoly and Vlad have helped me do a field assessment of all the leaders and as many other individuals as possible. Thirty are being escorted with the force traveling north, and they will travel farther north. They are a mix of battle fatigue sufferers and those leaders who were ousted for objecting to the assault." Olaf continued going over the details, the experience level, and the psychological state in his opinion.

Concluding, he said, "Morale is high. This is the best opportunity these people have ever had. That your force was detected two days into movement is a concern. Either they have forces out closer to you than I estimated, or they pushed patrols out from their borders. If we are pushed back from the assault, we will filter back to your position."

"It is a bad option, everyone knows it. But at least four partisan bands have been wiped out by the tank and its weapon. They have to act now to take out the base while the tank is out of immediate range on the base. We will leave for the assault in seventy-two hours. If you can push scouts out to confirm the tank force location, that would be appreciated. Suggest Were scouts along the highway."

Paul grunted, then said, "Confirm. Will send out a special group tonight. Will dig in at least twenty-four hours out from contact. Any additional information on the weapon?"

"Beyond the fact that it can target the shuttles before they can localize it? No. Do not use the shuttles to take it out. I have my only railgun with a team of Weres circling the base to take out the tank when it engages you. I hope they are in range before you engage."

"Understood. Will report your status to higher. Will try to obtain confirmation of tank route. Out." Paul finished with a sigh.

CHAPTER TWENTY

Paul had cut it close. Less than thirty minutes before the deadline Olaf had given him there had been a report of the tank. It was about thirty-six hours out from the main body of the relief force. They were digging in like wombats in place on his orders. He had two 30mm mortars that he had sent behind the scouts to perform a few shoot and scoots.

Firing from behind hills in a couple of places, they could hit and move out of the line of sight of the tank. With Weres defending them as they left, any patrol that ranged on them would be chewed up before they could take out the mortar teams.

And even if the mortar teams were killed, their presence would keep the focus of the tank force on Paul. If they headed back now, Paul was close enough to chew them up with harassment from the rear. They had to move forward, force an engagement.

The northern force was in position. The troops on the eastern flank should reach their assault point in the next thirty minutes. An hour after everyone was supposed to be in position the assault would begin—with the noonday sun. The Vampires might have a way to circumvent the usual sun sensitivity. Then again, they might not. Best to take every advantage they could.

Every survivor of encounters with Vampire-led patrols had reported them at night. Their plan had to form around that detail.

<<<>>>

In bear form, Olaf was waiting with a pair of partisans ready to cut the first layer of razor wire. He would have to wreck the second line with his body. No one would be able to keep up with him.

Waiting, he could hear every shuffle, every nervous movement, from the force behind him. He gritted his teeth at every sound. He knew the quiet sounds couldn't be carrying to the enemy. But every single rustle ratcheted up his nerves.

The minutes ticked by slowly. Oh, so slowly. Olaf must have looked tense, because the closest partisan murmured, "Fifteen minutes." How he wished it was Stasia or one of his men there. But, in the end, the guerrillas had requested they be spread among the groups as trained advisers.

Stasia had been picked to lead the southern assault group. It was the largest with a hundred and fifty stationed there. Olaf had a hundred and twenty-five in his own. The rest were in the Eastern group—the Fall-back position.

Suddenly, the silence broke with gunfire to the east. If he could have sworn, he would have. On a hair trigger, the two partisans moved up and clipped the wire. Then everyone else froze, even Olaf, as thirty men swarmed out of the bunkers.

He had been right. These men were no more disciplined than bandits. For all they knew, their returning patrol had been ambushed. The volume of gunfire to the east made it clear that there couldn't be more than thirty men firing in addition to the Fallback group.

Olaf held a paw to the side, and the assault group behind him froze. Straining his ears, he heard a single voice shouting, "Get back into position, soldiers! It could be a feint, damn it!"

But no-one stepped from the bunker to back it up.

Then a shot rang out, and someone near the front of the mob that had been moving to the gunfire fell. Over speakers in the compound went an amplified voice. "Return to your posts or be shot. Now!"

Olaf surged forward as the soldiers out of the bunkers hesitated. When he hit the second line of razor wire, he roared as it sliced into his paws. Even as thick as his hide was, it managed to cut. Still, he healed fast, and his roar had the additional advantage of making the undisciplined troops hesitate again.

He charged forward hard. His claws shredded the wire where he smashed it into the ground. His armored bulk crushed it to the ground, a satisfying feeling of metal straining and snapping as his weight stressed it beyond its limits.

Those with the wire cutters would widen it as the first assault team filtered through the gap he made.

Inside the base perimeter, Olaf quickly made out his target, the bunker back from the others. He could already hear sniper fire from his observation site. Two of the machine guns opened up on him, but he was moving faster than they could track.

The first assault team moved along the inside of the razor wire, half firing at the machine gun posts as the other half surged forward. The fire and maneuver tactics were utterly unnecessary. Distracted by the gunfire from the east, panicked by the bear in armor that had burst through the razor wire, they had tunneled in on Olaf. They charged as soon as they realized they were under no threat. The lead group charged the closet gun pit.

The snipers had already taken out the three gun-pits that they could target. They were now working on the troops frozen in shock at the carnage that had burst in amongst them.

The stench of death hung heavy over the entire base. It made

Olaf feel nauseous, but he focused on the task at hand. He was fast approaching the bunker. Rather than risk the door, he approached one of the vision slits in the side. Stomping on the charge, lightly for him, and he felt the trigger fuse break. He had about ten seconds before it blew. Knowing how fast he was, but not knowing how fast any Vampire inside might be, he counted to five.

'One bloody, two bloody, three bloody...'

Then he threw it in and started counting again. At two bloody, not having heard any movement, he moved away from the bunker as fast as he could. The explosives that Lilith had come up with were more powerful than C4. The amount used in the satchel charge was not 'just enough' kill—it was complete overkill. Even with the bunker walls to absorb most of the explosion, he didn't want to be too close when it went off.

He was over a hundred meters away when the charge went off. He was still thrown onto his face.

Sniffing the air, all he could smell was the Vampire stench of old, rotted, blood. Even the flame and explosive odor didn't penetrate it.

Olaf now knew why the observation point had never been found by the Vampires. They wouldn't have been able to identify individual scents that close over the stench of death that came from the reinforced cave entrance. The smell that could only come from a group of Vampires living there for decades.

And it was overwhelming. Olaf looked around and saw groups of soldiers assaulting the bunkers.

The dull thuds of grenades through the slits and groups of ten moving in to clear the bunkers could be seen.

Here and there he could see fallen partisans. At least twenty were down. Some were being aided by comrades. Others had people grieving over them. But the losses should have been higher. Luck had been on their side.

The gunfire from the east had finished sometime before his

hearing fully returned. He could see a figure trotting down the roadway towards them. He hoped the casualties had not been extensive in that group. He had deliberately placed most of those who showed signs of battle fatigue in it.

That left the cave. Olaf had to assume there were at least three Vampires in it. As well as an unknown number of Nosferatu. He wished there were at least *some* shotguns amongst his force. Invading those caves was going to get bloody. None of the AK variant rifles that both of his forces used were a particularly effective weapon in cave fighting, especially not in cave where they were fighting against Nosferatu.

<<<>>>

Olaf shifted back to human form to organize a group to assault the cave. Others from his platoon were organizing a team to take perimeter watch while seventy or more rifles were aimed at the entrance in short order.

All those involved had heard at least tales of the Nosferatu. The remaining Weres from his bodyguard approached him, as did several of the group leaders.

Before Olaf could even say a word, Anatoly said, "Don't even think of it, Olaf. We're coming. You are *not* walking into a cave with at least twenty, if not more, Nosferatu and probably three full Vamps alone."

Sighing, Olaf nodded. Then, after thinking about it, he said, "No more than fifteen in the lead group. Twenty in reserve. At least two Weres stay with the perimeter in case it takes until nightfall, and we have leakers. It seems that they either can't be out in the sunlight or have chosen to fight in the caves. Still, leaves us with the same problem. We have to fight them on their terms."

"There are lights in the caves," one of the other Weres said diffidently. "You can see the glow from them around the corner."

"We can't rely on lights being there the whole way. If that's all there is, I'm going ahead alone in the dark areas. I've trained for fighting hand-to-hand while blind. I doubt many in the group have. Besides, what if they turn them off to ambush us?"

"All the bodyguards have flashlights or gun lights," Anatoly reminded him.

"But we need some of them to stay with the perimeter force. We don't want to have to track down an escaped Vampire," Olaf responded.

Anatoly shrugged. "Have them trade with the assault group. All of them can use the 47s most of the partisans have. There aren't that many differences with the rifle we use. In a cave fight, it'll be trigger and bayonet anyways."

The group nodded grimly. Olaf said, "Get it organized, then we take it to these bloodsuckers. Now, I need something to eat before we begin."

CHAPTER TWENTY-ONE

Olaf was relieved to finally be in the cave and hunting. It should have taken fifteen minutes to get the assault team ready. Instead, it had taken nearly two hours. It seemed every single one of his bodyguard wanted to argue with him being the scout. Two had tried to show they could withstand it in wolf form.

They had ended up on the ground retching in disgust and writhing in pain from the stench coming from the cave. It was just too pungent for their animal form nose, and it would only get worse the farther into the cave they went.

Somehow, continued exposure was allowing Olaf to ignore it. With the modifications Lilith had made to his father's line, his sense of smell was not significantly weaker as a human compared to his bear form.

The biggest problem was that he could not smell anything else through it. Smell was not a particularly vital part of fighting blind, but it did feed into the other senses.

None of that changed the fact that he was the person in the group most suited to be scouting ahead. In his bear form, he could take more punishment than anyone else, and it was most likely that the Nosferatu would be sent ahead of their masters.

If they tried to feed on him, they would at least be incapacitated according to Lilith. Something about that amused him. But Olaf wished that she had made changes to the nanites in the other Weres. He knew that the programming had been modified before he was born, so they were no longer potentially lethal to other humans.

What had prevented her from giving other Shifters the same protection that he and his family enjoyed? Then again, maybe it had been a decision she had made on her own. After all, she was incredibly protective of them. At least in some peculiar ways.

She was perfectly happy for them to throw themselves into battle for their own reasons. But she wanted them as capable as possible when they went into a fight.

She wanted them to have every advantage, every edge, against anything else out there. Boris, on the other hand, would worry about any harm the modifications might cause those who carried them.

Olaf shook himself. He needed to stop philosophizing and get ready for what would probably be the most brutal fight of his life.

It would be the greatest risk he had ever faced. His other over-protector, his own father, had seen to that.

As the first team reached the entrance to the underground complex, Anatoly took him aside quietly, asking, "Are you sure you want to scout, boss? I know I already said most of my piece, but there is one factor that you need to consider. You are holding all this together. Oskar might be able to if things go truly awful down there. If Stasia wasn't going, she might be able to as well. But you are the one that has and can."

Olaf looked at him, honestly considering the argument. Most of the other arguments people put forward had been based on Olaf being critical because of who his father was.

This one made him reconsider them all in a different light. However, it was still missing a vital point. Olaf shook his head and said, "If we take catastrophic losses pulling these people out and I had stayed, people would turn away from me as a leader. There is no point in putting this off. No point in thinking there is another way. If I go down preventing catastrophic losses, my authority will devolve to you, Stasia, or Oskar. And it will be enhanced."

Taking a rigid stance, Olaf continued, "Besides, there isn't anyone else who could possibly take down a powerful Vampire. Not here. The closest one who might—*might*—be able to do as good a job as I can is Paul. And there is no way whatever is in there is gonna wait a week or more for more troops to get here. Even if Paul does manage to take out the tank with its accompanying force."

Anatoly nodded and let Olaf pass him. Once he was at the cave entrance, he shifted. They had managed to find a dozen shotguns for the assault teams in the bunkers and above ground camps, as well as six, thirty round magazines for each of the scavenged AA-12s.

The shotguns were to be at least twenty meters behind him. They had flashlights duct taped to the barrels. How there was still viable and working duct tape around the camp had been beyond everyone, but as a field expedient, it would do the job for long enough.

They had been right to be worried about the lights. The ones at the front of the complex were on, but the rest of the system was pitch black. It was the small things that complicated life and combat. Boris pushed a little further forward than they had discussed. In the dark, humans would need more warning. Even with the flashlights, there was only so much that they could illuminate.

To be honest, Olaf would have preferred there to be no flashlights at all. Mostly, he would have preferred to go in alone. That would not have flown well with his allies, or his bodyguards, however. Besides, even if he could not defeat the Vampire inside, he might be able to weaken it enough that humans with guns would be able to finish it off.

Now was not the time to be proud. Now was the time to be a leader.

The tunnels led straight into an unoccupied series of guard rooms, ready rooms, and barracks with an armory. The beds were unkept, but the room was clean. They were all empty as well. It seemed the supposition of the enemy emptying the base was correct. There was even a handy-dandy map in one of the ready rooms. One that it became clear they could not trust after the first fifty meters beyond the barracks.

They did find one useful thing in the ready rooms, a box of road flares. Unsure if they would work after sixty or so years, Anatoly and Stasia worked them into the planning in addition to the flashlights, rather than instead of.

Behind the barracks was a maze of tunnels and rooms. Most of them were apparently Post-Fall additions. Rather than plaster over the rock, there was just bare worked stone that had been carved out of the hill with a pickaxe.

Olaf hated to think of the work involved in burrowing out this mountain like that. It could be done. It had been done before the rise of technology long before the Fall. This was an example of old methods being used again.

The storerooms were full of foodstuffs and looted materials. Grains, tanned hides, smoked meats, the works. This group was getting fat on the supply side. Olaf had a sinking feeling that they had hit the western edge of Raina's territory, and that such a stockpile being located there spoke of the size of the lands between there and his relief force—or at least the territory of which she had control.

There was too much for pure raiding. They had to have people they extracted tribute from.

Raina had to be stripping her subjects to the absolute

minimum to have such resources. The suffering her people had to be enduring started a fire in Olaf's mind.

The nature of the mountainous terrain, and the kinds of people it attracted, may have proven too much for her to overcome without more effort than she wanted to expend. Hunting down every band along her borders would have been a near-impossible task. Hunting down every bandit band had been beyond Boris. Raina's brutality had caused the entire remaining population of that region to turn on her with a burning, toxic, hatred.

But the sheer number of rooms complicated things enormously. Olaf was growing frustrated with the constant diversions down side corridors. The second team had moved up closer, clearing two out of three of the side passages as they moved deeper into the complex.

'One thing all this does was to make sure the enemy knew someone was coming,' Olaf mused to himself as he continued padding forward, 'I wonder if that was the plan all along, or if it was simply a beneficial side effect?'

He picked up the pace, and the first assault team had to ignore their designated side passages to keep up. They were still falling behind him. They had been down there for at least half an hour. Everyone was getting tense, and the batteries in the flashlights wouldn't last forever.

Olaf just wanted the day to be over. He needed to dig that nest of nastiness out. He was distracted by his frustration and impatience when the Nosferatu finally did strike.

A swarm of at least ten piled straight in on him. Pushing him to the side, their numbers made it impossible for him to block the entire tunnel from the others who streamed past. With a roar, Olaf started slashing at and biting into the mound of Nosferatu that had piled into him.

Even above his roar could be heard the shrieks and hunger-driven cries of the Nosferatu. Shouts of encouragement and orders from both Stasia and Anatoly could be heard echoing back down the cave.

Olaf could already hear the shotguns firing behind him. He had to wonder how effective they were. Fear for those under his command took over, and he went into a blind rage. These monsters were after people he cared for. They would not stop him from helping them.

His jaws clamped down on the closet body part, and he shook the Nosferatu ferociously. The nearest half-dozen were knocked back like bowling pins as his fury took hold. The body part, a leg, tore out of his target's hip socket, and the human-shaped missile knocked over several more causing a jam, one he could hopefully hold back while the others dealt with the half-dozen or so leakers.

The taste of the blood in his mouth was foul and distracted him for long enough that one of the Nosferatu that had been surrounding him managed to bite. Shortly afterward, he felt the fangs fall out of his thigh.

The world seemed to pause as it let loose a banshee scream of pain. Afterwards, there was a moment of absolute silence. What-ever had happened had frozen the other Nosferatu briefly. Olaf took advantage of whatever had happened. He started mauling those still around him with both paws. Gaining fighting room away from the wall he had been pushed against.

Forcing them to go through him before they could reach those under his command. His determination solidified, and the sound of gunfire moved closer. His backup would get here soon. He just had to hold his position.

He swung back and forth to slam the Nosferatu back with jabs and swipes of his paws. Grabbing one with a lunge and a bite, he used it as a bludgeon against its fellows. He held his posi-tion. Held his ground. The gunfire behind him kept chattering. Some of his assault team was still standing, still fighting those that did get past him.

Another Nosferatu managed to sink its teeth into him, this time into his wrist just above his paw. Within seconds it was violently seizing. He was forced to shatter the monster's head into the floor to get it off his arm. The body went limp as the skull was pulverized.

The short time it took him to disentangle himself was enough for another to slip past, but he was more worried about the mass. While he had injured several and killed at least five, he couldn't see the end of them. It was too dark to see past the first rank of his foes.

Then the support arrived. A wall of fire sent out a wall of lead above Olaf's head. In their tightly packed situation, the Nosferatu could not dodge, nor was there time to flee from the avalanche of lead.

In less than a minute, they were all down, and Olaf was trying to spit their foul-tasting blood out of his mouth.

Anatoly approached a little cautiously and figured out what Olaf was trying to do. He pulled out a canteen of water and poured some of it over Olaf's muzzle. Olaf looked at him and angled his mouth to get some more to wash his mouth out with.

Anatoly paused the pour, certain he had Olaf's full attention. "I told you we should have been closer." Olaf flashed a reproachful look back at Anatoly, inasmuch as a bear can look reproachful. Then the water poured, and Olaf managed to wash out his mouth.

The first, and least dangerous, part of infiltrating the complex was complete.

CHAPTER TWENTY-TWO

Olaf's body slumped slightly in fatigue after the last of the Nosferatu went down. Shots sounded out around him as partisans made sure the Nosferatu were dead for good. He could feel the grief building in some, converting to rage in others. His forces had taken the brunt of the attack. In at least one case, from the fall of bodies, one of his bodyguard detail had sacrificed himself to protect two partisans from the enemy.

He was sick of it. Alone, he could have defeated those monsters. Giving them more prey had been a mistake. Giving Raina more prey would be a similar mistake. Anatoly was down, injured. Oskar and Stasia had taken over organizing the treatment of the wounded. If he was going to prevent more unnecessary casualties, he needed to move now.

Olaf was determined to take out the Vampire only he had a chance against. After moving along the corridor as to prevent a surprise attack, he lay on the ground. In the middle of the passageway, his bulk was an effective stopper.

Olaf waited patiently. More than half of the forty in the assault group were injured or dead. From what he had seen, twelve of his bodyguards were among the fallen. A horrific price to pay.

Yet not as high as fighting them in the open would have been. Olaf had to wonder why the Nosferatu had been held back. The confinement of the tunnels had given his troops a decisive advantage.

Then again, they were bloodthirsty horrors. Perhaps they could not be controlled well enough for the Vampire to risk setting them loose with her troops in the field? Olaf kept his focus on the corridor ahead and waved off one of the troopers doing triage assessments when they finally had time to check him for wounds.

He had been waiting for that moment. Then he stood and hurried off, getting far enough ahead of his allies while they were distracted. No more of them needed to be endangered. He would deal with the problem—with Raina—personally.

<<<>>>

It was at least ten minutes later when Stasia looked down the corridor expecting to see Olaf. She had expected to see him on the floor, lying down as a guard and tunnel block. He was gone. Swearing, Stasia yelled down the hall, "Oskar! Olaf has gone. Gather the security detail. We need to go after him. We *can't* let him face that bitch alone."

Oskar looked at her, slight confusion on his face. "It's gonna be a battle of the Titans, Stasia. I would not have believed anyone could take on twenty or thirty of these fiends and live! The fact that Olaf even has the energy to move after such a fight surprises me. That tells me it's entirely possible that he's doing the right thing."

Stasia snorted and shook her head in disgust, "do you think he will be facing her alone? If there is anyone else there, we will at least help even the odds."

Oskar stood there for a moment after thinking about it. He gave even odds to her being alone. If she was powerful enough, she could have believed the force Olaf led was unworthy of her attention. If they managed to reach her anyways, then they were replacements for her losses, in her mind. Why waste energy on opponents not worthy of notice?

And that was if she saw herself as part of the military force. If she saw herself as more of a civil head, then she could justify sending whatever forces were at hand before facing the attackers after all. Why else have a military force?

But Stasia had a point. If Raina did have remaining forces, Boris would be at an extreme disadvantage. Everyone still in the tunnel was already in a risky situation. Sighing, he nodded and shouted, "Viktor, Terus, Delmar, George, Hugo! Grab a shotgun and load up on ammo. We need to at least try and save his furry and stupid hide." Stasia started to head off down the tunnel. Impatience getting the better of her, but an angry hand clamped down on a shoulder.

"No," Oskar ground out. An aura of command surrounded him. "We go together, or not at all. If we come in one at the time, we will be a liability."

Stasia turned a burning glare on him, but he just shook his head. Stasia let her gaze fall and sighed with regret. After two minutes, the rescue team was ready and headed out.

<<<>>>

Olaf had made turns down doglegs and around corners. There seemed to be no reason for them. There were no more storage rooms, but he felt like they had doubled back around, and that he was near the center of the area the enemy base had been on.

He grimaced as he detected ten or more etheric sources ahead. He could not believe that there were ten Vampires ahead.

Besides, all but one of them felt wrong. As if they were oily compared to the clean water he was used to. But for him to even be detecting one was a bad sign. He had not felt the Nos, and the tank had only been on the edge of the range he could usually sense them on. His mother and his father were the only people he had ever sensed before.

Paul and Alexi simply did not have a large enough signature for him to feel. The shuttle engines and the main generator he could sense at about three or four kilometers. That was one of the reasons the shuttle had been used. It had sensors that were much more sensitive than the one in his skull.

As he approached one of the doorways, he felt the smallest signature rise and peak. Instinctively, he dove his bear form through, rolling to get quickly back on his feet. He saw a jagged red lance of energy pass over his head and smelled the acrid odor of ozone. A bitter taste filled his mouth as he realized how close the bolt had come to hitting. The scent of scorched fur from the heat of the blast filled the room, overwhelming the smell of death for a time.

He tensed as he heard a trigger click, but there was no accompanying arc of energy or spike in the etheric signature. A snarl filled the room, followed by cursing. "Cocklicking useless test. What a cluster fuck. And a Wechselbalg would have been the perfect subject. If it works on one of you, it will work on anyone."

Looking up, he saw no one else in the antechamber. As he rose, the Vampire was already moving towards him. He was barely fast enough to turn a potentially lethal kick into a glancing blow across his back leg. It still hurt.

Olaf sent a mauling back at Raina, who rode the blow enough to only receive shallow scratches. Both now on their feet and aware that they were roughly the same speed. Olaf glanced around the room. It had a double door that was open to what looked like an underground military vehicle park. The eight remaining signatures were beyond it, unmoving.

The room itself was large, easily forty meters by forty meters. Olaf quickly learned to follow her movement more carefully. A kick to the ribs showed that any distraction could cost him. A sharp crack in her foot told Raina that any personal attacks against Olaf would also extract a price.

His reflexive counterstrike had barely glanced off her foot, but he had managed to break something. It healed quickly, but it encouraged Raina to go on the defensive. She needed to keep him at bay until her sidearm recharged. It should have been good for two or three shots before needing to charge. She had been a little hard on the trigger this time.

They fought back and forth, rarely landing a blow. Their fight covered most of the room, with Olaf knocking over tables in his frustration at being unable to reach her. Raina was desperately hoping that she was tiring the Werebear out. Tension simmered in the room when the deadlock was broken.

Eight armed figures burst into the room. As they raised their weapons, Raina desperately dodged behind concrete plinths that had held steel desktops before Olaf had knocked them off.

Thunder barked. An Armageddon of bullets, slugs, and buckshot filled the air around her. One of the slugs from the AA-12s hit, spinning her as she dove behind the cover of the concrete. What had been a solid meter by two-meter block became pockmarked and chipped as bullets and buckshot peppered it.

The interlopers spread slowly, those with empty magazines reloading first, then those with partial loads following suit. A quiet beep seemed to echo in the near silence left by the lull in the gunfire. Raina looked longingly at the vehicle hanger. She could have evaded even that many attackers there, but flashing through the etheric with her sidearm charged could be a problem.

The etheric and the energy the weapon drew on did not mix. It was close to the etheric energy pods she had discovered how to create, but it was hungrier. That was what made blasts of it a more viable, and targeted, weapon. She heard the bear approaching, but she was not sure the energy would arc from the Were to the others. It might arc from one of them to the next, servicing many of her foes in a single shot.

Risking a glance, she saw one of them was female. A smile took her face. Killing her would make any survivors either grieve or become enraged. Either way, it would make them easier to kill. Quickly rising on the other side of the concrete, she took her shot.

Olaf saw her rising, lifting the gun faster than his allies could react. He could see her target, and his heart shredded. Desperately, he charged across, placing his body in the path of the bolt. The smell of burning fur and cooking flesh filled the air, and pain quickly became all he knew.

Then, Raina disappeared. Her voice could be heard, a shout ringing out in triumph. With that damned Werebear out of the way, she could cleanse the base of those who would dare defy her. It might take time, but she now had a chance

Olaf writhed as the vicious energy surged through him. For the first time in his life, he felt an unexpected change happening. His legs lengthened, his hip joints shifted. His form became the one in between man and beast, that of the Pricolici.

He roared as the change continued, painfully shedding the burnt flesh from his body as it shifted in a manner most unusual for a shifter. Rather than the fast change, it was slow, and painful because of the decreased speed of the change. Roars of pain and rage echoed throughout the base as he pulled himself to his feet. Stalking into the vehicle park, he was struck by a hail of bullets from an assault rifle. None were silver, so none of them did any permanent harm.

Olaf's allies stared in shock at what he had become. "Stay herrre," he growled over his shoulder at them.

This was his fight. He would kill the bitch that had tried to kill the first woman that had held an interest in him as a person.

That had not cared who his father was, but had judged him only on his actions.

Fury walked with every step. Fear rode out from him in waves. His troops took defensive positions in the room he left. Preparing to shoot whichever monster came back through the door.

Raina was hiding behind a tank. Her mind raced, wondering what had happened. It had been at least five centuries since she had heard of a Wechselbalg taking that form. She now wished she had a better mastery of flashing through the etheric. Even the small step she had taken had exhausted her.

Olaf could feel her. She was hiding behind the chassis of a T-72. He stalked towards her, letting the fear settle in. Her signature was the only clean one in the room. Eight massive fixtures, replacement turrets for the tanks in the hanger, had the other signatures.

Fear gnawed at Raina. She had never felt anything like the presence coming from this being. As she rose from her hiding spot, she desperately searched for another weapon to replace the empty assault rifle.

She had no silver. She was facing a Pricolici in a rage. She needed some way of dealing massive damage in a single effort. Her experimental pistol would be worse than useless. For all she knew, it would only make the monster even worse.

Her plans were ashes. She had used harsh methods, but she had been trying to find a way to help humanity rebuild, to become their saviour. If that meant she had to rule the rabble they had become, it was for their own good.

Now, despair filled her. She couldn't escape the monster stalking her. Her quest for power and domination was over. But she was one of the oldest vampires there. She could still die with honor. She rose from her place of concealment and exposed herself to the Pricolici. She could still die on her feet.

In an act of mercy from the universe, she did not feel the blow when it landed.

CHAPTER TWENTY-THREE

After some risky scouting into the city, the plans on which buildings to assault had changed. There was a cluster of three still-standing Soviet-era skyscrapers that were closer to fortified strong points than anything else in the city. All of them were strongly defended at the base. However, the placement of civilians as 'human shields' showed that there was no real planning against an air assault from the shuttles.

Perhaps their enemies were unaware of the presence of the crafts. Perhaps they believed Boris would not put them at any risk. To be fair, Boris would not risk them. However, there was nothing that Viktor had used from his arsenal that could harm the shuttles. There had been a few surprises, but nothing that extraordinary.

So, after longer than Boris liked, his forces were ready to assault the towers. Their biggest problem would be opening the rusty roof hatches with a modicum of silence. The Soviet construction may be ugly as hell, but it was solid.

Once those towers were properly manned, taking them back would be hell for the enemy. Even if they managed to—something Boris believed they lacked the training and morale to achieve—their losses would be hideous. He would land a company on each, have the first platoon infiltrate down five or six floors, and leave a white phosphorus surprise to give the defenders something to distract them.

If the hatch were too rusted, it would be quieter to thermite open the hatches. There seemed to be a few sharpshooters in the upper floors, but no defenders otherwise. His biggest concern was the civilian 'hostages.'

There were enough of them that he was seriously worried about causing casualties, but taking the towers would shorten the siege considerably. Boris desperately hoped he could do something to reduce the food shortages for them. Too many people had already been killed. If Viktor had not been so insane, so abusive and expansionist, Boris would have left well enough alone.

But a wise leader did not leave a rabid beast next door. Like any form of a rabid animal, there was only one wise choice with Viktor. A bullet to the brainpan.

Boris was just disappointed that he could not be part of the initial assault. He was moving in after the towers and central area between them had been cleared. Two regiments of his would man the salient. The Swedes had landed a regiment of Marines, and the Finns had sent three times the forces they had initially agreed to send.

Apparently, Viktor had tried raiding their lands as well. He had not even been looking towards Arkhangelsk Palden. Boris was not sure if Viktor's actions represented overambition or active stupidity.

Viktor was outnumbered more than three to one in troops. When it came to artillery, he equalled the mortars of Boris's force, but had fewer field guns and nothing to match the crude howitzers Boris had pulled together.

If his forces could take and hold those towers, then Boris was grimly satisfied they could crush Viktor's forces. Even if the combined positions did not force an outright surrender.

And if he could not go in, at least he had the Arkhangelsk Regiment. They trained for it, and Mark was an intelligent officer. Boris was sure he was the second-best choice, but Janna had delivered an ultimatum. If Boris led the assault on any tower, she was leading the assault on one of the other two.

Now, all Boris could do was wait. Wait and depend on the skill of the soldiers he was sending into battle and depend on the planning that had gone into the assault.

<<<>>>

Gregori was impatiently waiting for his man to burn through the hinges on the hatch. Over the decades since someone had last opened it, the hinges had rusted shut. At least it was a contingency that was within the plans. The thermite lance they were using was crude. Just smoked autumn venison compressed around an aluminum oxide core. But it was doing the job nicely.

The windmill and the radio mast indicated they would have people two floors down. Possibly people on the top floor. Someone had to maintain the bloody things.

Once the hatch was open, a security team of four rushed down the ladder. The task Gregori's platoon faced was an initial clearance of the top floor. That would allow them to deploy the battalion in the top few floors before fighting their way down.

Three armored Shifters in wolf form were the next down, scouting the vicinity quickly and effectively as the remainder made their way through the open hatchway. They knew the enemy had silver rounds, but Shifters made better scouts than anyone else. They could also move faster and were experts at silent takedowns.

They would be on the front of the spear for every second floor once the battalion deployed, with other elements securing the floors after they were cleared. The top floor had been empty, except for a pair of chatting guards the Were scouts localized and quickly killed. They had been sitting down and chatting with their weapons clear of their bodies. Boredom and routine had clearly set in among at least some of the troops in the tower.

He could not rely on that. In fact, when clearing the second floor, they encountered a guarded door. The guard next to it was alert and scanning the hallway doors. Fortunately, a Shifter had smelled the unwashed man before turning the corner. Using the body signals to indicate the problem, the man had retrieved a mirror to see what the issue was.

As the guard was stationary, a quick burst from the silenced BIZON had been enough to take him down with minimal noise.

The low electric light over the door had exposed the sentry by silhouetting him slightly and had not been strong enough to betray the small movement in the corner twenty meters down the hallway.

As they approached the door, it became clear why there had been no alarm. Even at this time of night, sounds of the radio watch were loud through the door.

Gregori brought up the reserve squad as soon as the Shifter reached him. The comms unit would have to be on this floor or the next. That it was here meant they had to take it out quickly, quietly, and hope no transmission was interrupted.

That could give away the assault to those lower down. The squad's leader, Ivan, had pointed out a bundle of cabling and wires leading to the nearby elevator door. After backing up to the corridor, they held a quick, whispered conference.

They decided the best option was to cut the wires and hope they did not give the enemy advance warning. They would set a door charge on the door frame. The idiots had set the solid steel door into the original aluminum door frame.

Two troops pulled the corpse away as Doc set the charge. Probably the oldest member of the platoon, Doc was a Were who had both medic and explosive ordinance training. Some of the platoon joked that he could disarm a nuke in under a minute.

Once the broad-shouldered Doc had set the charge on the frame, he moved back and hand-signalled a three count. On one, the cabling was cut. On two, the entry team turned their backs on the door. With the boom, they turned back around, kicked the door in, and entered the room.

Most of the techs in the room started backing up at the sight of men with ready guns charging into the room. The unexpected concussion of the blast had startled most of them. One near a radio transmission set reached quickly for his gun. His head blew apart, a red mist mixed with shards of bone and gelatinous brain matter sprayed the man next to him and covered the equipment he had been standing against.

"On the floor! On the floor!" Gregori ordered loudly.

Four more men, out of the twenty in the room, either did not follow orders well, or did not move fast enough. Quick bursts from the entry group's weapons to chests and heads took down those four men, making the rest downright cheerful about being face down on the floor.

After quickly securing the survivors and sending them up, under guard, to a room on the top floor they had designated for prisoners, the platoon took a rest at their designated stairwell.

Having cleared the eighteenth floor, Third platoon, Second company, leap-frogged their position, leaving them in reserve and giving them a rest from the tension and stress of clearing a floor. Clearing a building this size took too long to leave a single force at the front. Everything went smoothly until they arrived at the fourth floor. Kills and captures of targets had required minimal gunfire.

The sounds of gunfire exploded in the direction of the north corridor to the corridor stairwell. Gregori said, "We've hit something," before moving towards the north on instinct. Then he paused, turned, and pointed to Petra. "Get your butt up to

Second company HQ," said the grizzled sergeant. "Get them to cover the stairwell. The third floor had to have heard that shit!"

As soon as she spun around in response, she shouted orders. Gregori started organizing troops, preparing them to move in assault formation towards the sound of gunfire. "You know what uniforms they are in. Shoot them, don't shoot ours," he snarled, sending the wolf and troop partners forward first.

The wolf/troop combination tactic was one Boris's forces often used. While the trooper distracted or pinned down the enemy forces, the wolves would get in close to rip at hamstrings and throats. If the enemy targeted the wolves, then the troops took them out with gunfire.

It was a brutal assault tactic that, when combined with the Werewolves abilities to heal fast, invariably lead to heavy enemy casualties inside positional defenses. The major problem was the casualties that it could accrue when facing layered defenses.

Defenses exactly like the ones they had encountered there. It was still more effective than a standard assault.

Still, Boris's forces had a joke. 'Who needs grenades when you've got Werewolves?'

That's not to say that they did not carry grenades, just that they used them less often than most forces. And today would be one of those days that they needed them.

The defenders had set up a defense in depth. There were three rows of sandbags with defenders posted both behind the sandbags and behind doorways and walls. The sandbag defenses buffered and supplemented.

The fighting was bloody as enemy troopers turned to face the new threat that Gregori's platoon presented, adding more defenders to those already facing their attack. Even under the relentless fire of twenty men, the Werewolves of Gregori's platoon were targeted.

Several of them went down with wounds from silver ammunition. The human troopers started moving forward under fire and maneuver, giving the remaining uninjured Weres an opportunity to find whatever cover they could.

Three more of his troops went down, but they had advanced twenty meters. Everyone had been able to take cover. With hand signals, Gregori informed his troops to pair up and ready covering fire and grenades. Due to the range in the inevitable stability of close combat in these circumstances, he also ordered them to fix bayonets

Gregori started a five count. On three, two of the troopers knelt out from cover and started pouring fire towards the barricades. On four, grenades could be heard exploding around the corner, a fortuitous attack from allied forces. With five, his soldiers armed and threw their grenades into the barricades. Then all troops took cover again, waiting for the cracks of the grenades.

They only had to wait a few seconds, and with the cracks came screams of agony from those enemy soldiers that had not managed to find cover from the explosions and shrapnel. Even those who had managed to find cover was stunned by the effects of near simultaneous grenade attacks from different axes of advance.

The conditions were perfect. The enemy was disorganized, and there was a slight smoke haze from the grenades. Gregori ordered a bayonet charge.

His troops leapt forward, the Werewolves joining the charge as friendly forces passed where they had found cover or had been feigning death. The vicious snarls of the Wolves joined with the bellowed howls of the blood-hungry soldiers.

Knife and fang pierced soft flesh, bayonet and claw lunged forth. Fist and rifle-butt hammered bodies on both sides. All these and more flashed and thudded, thumped and crashed as the forward barricades were overrun.

More of the enemy flowed towards the breached lines of

sandbags, but they arrived too late. Gregori and his men were already in amongst them.

Cries of despair and acts of suicidal defiance on the part of the enemy took place over the final stages of this battle. Gregori found himself without his rifle, face-to-face with a scar-faced, muscular, one-eyed man. Quickly drawing his hatchet, he parried the first bayonet strike, forcing it down, following the parry with a quick kick to the side of his scarred enemy's knee.

His opponent grunted, shifting his balance to the other leg slightly. Then the stocky opponent returned the favor with the butt stroke to the rib cage that landed with crushing force. There was no way to move in this dip among the improvised fortifications. What little fighting room they had was not enough to disengage or circle. His opponent recovered quickly, stabbing the bayonet towards Gregori's guts, and with the hatchet out of position for a good parry.

Forced to sweep the hatchet quickly up while ducking, hoping he could get enough force into the parry to avoid the blow, Gregori found himself gaining a massive opening. The hammer back of his hatchet was in perfect line for backswing to his opponent's head. It landed before he saw the opening.

His opponent didn't have time to react before his eyes glazed over, and he slumped silently to the ground.

All around him the sounds of actual fighting were quieting down. Quickly, they were replaced with the groans of the injured and the screams of the mortally wounded. The stench of blood and ruptured guts hit Gregori, and he collapsed to his knees as a weariness flowed over him. He had been clearing the building floor by floor for hours by now.

This fight had taken more energy than he had expected out of him. He hoped the rest of his unit did not feel the same way, although he suspected they did. If the remaining floors were this tightly defended, he was not sure that even the forces that had been committed to the assault would be enough to take the tower.

<<<>>>

Boris found himself looking down over St. Petersburg from the roof of the third tower. The fourth Battalion of the first Regiment had captured it, and a whole extra Regiment had completed landing and security in perimeter lines connecting the three towers. Although there was still some fighting going on in tower two, the operation could be considered a success once companies had finished sweeping the area contained within the perimeter.

Viktor would have to surrender. That or find out that he simply did not have the forces to fight two fronts. With a reinforced salient inside his lines that could sally in response to an assault from outside his lines, he had one place to go if he kept fighting.

Hell.

Now, all he waited for was for the sweep inside his own perimeter to finish so that he could set up a command post.

He was already relieved to see that civilians, who had escaped the clutches of whatever portion of Viktor's forces were holding them, were already being evacuated out past the siege lines by his shuttles. That meant that all the captives had already been taken away to the prisoner of war cage.

He was relieved that he finally had the freedom of action to help the innocent victims of this dreary conflict.

CHAPTER TWENTY-FOUR

Boris woke suddenly to the sound of close gunfire. He was momentarily disorientated. After capturing the three towers, his forces had swept the area. The towers made natural strongpoints for a perimeter. His command post was near the middle of the captured and cleared land.

There should not have been a penetration that deep into the salient. The perimeter was adequately manned, his soldiers were well-trained, and Viktor was still off balance after the attack.

His body reacted, as was to be expected from someone who was a veteran of so many wars. Rolling off his cot, grabbing for his rifle, Boris charged out of the room.

His camp had been lightly fortified.

Reacting as soon as he saw an enemy, identifying them by the differing quality of uniform and the missing armor, he fired a burst into them. Simply firing at the enemy would not be enough. His command post was just a little too isolated from the frontline and the reserve positions.

Even an old, experienced soldier could sometimes make a mistake.

There was only one real solution to the situation he found

himself in. Ducking behind a pitted, ruined concrete slab wall, Boris started to change. Only the strength and resilience of his beastman form would allow him to salvage any of his command group for this attack.

His self-anger and disappointment at having made the mistake that allowed this attack, whatever they were, morphed into a burning, seething, rage as he changed to the form he usually avoided.

With an earth-shattering roar, he burst into the focal point of the enemy attack. They had targeted the best-defended building. Perhaps they had assumed that had been where he was sleeping. Unfortunately for them, it was his communications center, with always active guards and messengers, and therefore the best-defended site in the command post.

That had slowed the assault just enough for Boris to reach it before the enemy could enter the building. His gallant soldiers had brought the time he needed to charge their rear with their blood and their lives.

Bodies flew clear in a maelstrom. The violence and destruction he inflicted on the rear ranks was immense. Shattering damage had been done before the enemy force all knew he was there. Limbs were torn off, and bodies smashed into ruin against the blighted city ground. Skulls shattered as strong men landed against the fractured concrete.

It had been a decade or more since Boris had found it necessary to take this form in combat. The reserve troops paused in shock and awe at the carnage he generated through the enemy formation. As the rear lines fell, the waning support from behind caused the assault by the front ranks to falter.

The loss of their fellows in the moans and screams beyond those normal, even in violent combat, gave them pause. Those who turned to face the carnage froze again at the nightmare, the blood covered bear-man, behind them. Those pauses were all it took for the reserve force to regain their equilibrium and fire a fusillade of bullets into the remaining forces, cutting them down like wheat at harvest.

His most elemental fury and anger satisfied, Boris managed to regain enough control to shift back into his human form. He did so with a shudder. After so long since he had taken that form in combat, he had forgotten the extra call it made, practically begging him to stay in it. He looked down at his wrecked uniform, then shrugged. He had things that needed to be done first.

He started barking out orders, Weres in wolf form gathered to track the sense of the attackers back to whichever hole they had come out of. Perhaps the raiders had managed to hide away, only to find themselves encircled. Enough of Viktor's forces had been left in place to harass Boris and his men during the advance. Attacking hidden bases, the intention had been to disorder his advance. It was possible the sole intention of this raid had been to cause chaos.

Then again, perhaps it was something else altogether.

A fire team of five Werewolves quickly gathered to Boris's infuriated orders. As he cursed and harassed his tired troops out of shock and back into an organized force, the Procolici started tracking the trail such a large party of men would have to have left.

Under the stern eye of his bodyguards, he hurried to his quarters to pull on a fresh uniform. After a scowl from the one that had followed him to his quarters, he grabbed his personal heavy combat armor and donned it as well.

Even a commander could have tyrants that gave him orders in their own subtle way.

<<<>>>

Boris shook his head as one of the Weres reported back. They had found precisely where the enemy force had infiltrated their lines.

It was an old sewerage line. No one had cleared it or secured it because most of the sewage lines in the occupied sections of St. Petersburg were above ground. Almost medieval in nature. His forces, himself included, had believed that the old sewer lines were useless because they could not have remained intact.

This one was intact enough to allow passage underneath both perimeters to behind his lines.

But if it allowed passage inside his lines, it might provide a route deep inside Viktor's defenses.

It was with some relief that Boris realized that he had to act now. He did not have the time to consult Danislav or Janna if he wanted to take the risk or, as he preferred to think of it, grasp this opportunity which had been presented to him.

He had to organize a penetration force now. After considering the defenses and their needs, he gathered up platoons to make a company. That was all he could afford to pull from the towers and the perimeter. Then he ordered a company pulled from the reserve regiment for the raid. It would take about an hour to gather them.

From the forces that made his bodyguard, about two platoons had followed him to the entrance that the Wolves had found. He selected five troopers. They, along with the Shifters, would scout the sewer tunnel, and check if the exit was guarded.

Boris had his doubts that it would be, as Viktor seemed to lack the training of his father or the experience of his grandfather. Neither of them would have risked an enemy having an unguarded sally port. Both of them would have defended the upper floors of those Soviet towers to a far greater extent than Viktor had.

As forces gathered, the tension amongst them ratcheted up. A successful raid would throw their opponents even more off balance. It would allow his forces to dictate the pace of combat.

But given the direction this tunnel headed, Boris had hopes of an even more significant breakthrough.

Several of the escaped civilians had revealed a probable location for Viktor's headquarters when they were debriefed. Before they were sent outside of the city. Depending on where the tunnel exited, it could allow an actual assault on his headquarters. An opportunity to pull off a successful raid on the enemy command post as a riposte to the unsuccessful raid against his own.

Other methods at hand had been considered for taking out that site. Each had disadvantages severe enough to cause their abandonment.

Bombardment was a problem due to a combination of distance and the heavy overhead cover of Viktor's chosen command post. Even though the heaviest howitzer shells could range in on it, there was no guarantee they could penetrate the heavy concrete that made the roof of the complex. Any bombardment would warn him that they had pinpointed his command post, and therefore the entire concept had been dropped.

Air assaults had also been considered, but Viktor had broken out anti-aircraft weaponry after those towers had been taken. Despite the age of the weapons, they could well take down the shuttle while it was landing troops.

The Gravitic engines had to be shut down to allow troops, especially unenhanced troops, to disembark safely. While the shuttles were adept at hovering on thrusters alone, they were vulnerable when deploying troops due to the requirements of a stable rappelling platform.

However, if Viktor had been careless enough to leave no guards, or even too few guards, on the exit to the sewer tunnel, it presented an opportunity Boris could not ignore.

An underground passageway offered his forces an opportunity, the same opportunity Viktor had seen, to penetrate the enemy lines. Boris's forces simply had not considered it because the sewage channels and other underground conduits had seemed derelict when they first investigated them.

<<<>>>

His forward team had managed to take down the four guards that has been left on the sewer exit without attracting attention. Deploying more than two companies through the small exit without attracting attention from the patrols had been a more difficult challenge.

In fact, in the end, they had been forced to stalk and eliminate one of the patrols. That unit passed over near the tunnel entrance too regularly for a covert deployment of any significant force to be successful.

Knives and silenced pistols had managed the task efficiently and effectively.

Rather than bull their way through towards the command post, Boris's forces moved stealthily, silently, flitting from cover to cover like ghosts in the night. That had been the downfall of Viktor's attack. His forces had gone in without regard to the noise they might make and any forces that might be attracted to it.

Once they were in clear sight of the watch post, Boris started detaching marksman and sniper teams. The command post and surrounding areas were heavily patrolled, but there was only so much fortification possible in this ruined city. Although this area was in better condition than the portion Boris had captured, many of the buildings were crumbling.

Boris pushed on after the detachments with the bulk of his forces, preparing to assault the main entryway. Two platoons of troops were detached. Moving around the patrolled perimeter, they were to complete the encirclement of the command post. Doing so would ensure no escape was possible.

He was still concerned about the possibility of Viktor

escaping with a significant number of loyal followers. That would allow Viktor to continue to cause problems for everyone, both in St. Petersburg and elsewhere in the realms.

His actions already showed he had the mindset of a bandit or raider rather than those of a true ruler. Now, Boris had to wait while his forces infiltrated and proceeded into position. The lieutenant in command of the platoon and responsible for covering the rear of the command post would send up a green flare when his forces were in place. That was when Boris would launch his assault.

Now, all that was left for Boris and the assault force was a long, nervous, wait.

<<<>>>

Tension filled the air. Boris forced himself to remain still as the time he estimated his platoons should have taken to gain their positions passed. Nervous tension filled him like a tightening spring, but outwardly, his face showed a confident and imperturbable calm. His troops did not need his nervousness to add to their own.

There was a quiet hiss and pop as the flare finally brightened the slightly greying sky. Dawn could not be far off. As soon as they saw it, his troops leapt into action with Boris near the head of the charge. While he would prefer to have been at the head of the charge, his bodyguards had managed to position themselves so as to make that impossible.

Sniper shots cracked loudly, breaking the silence of the night. Guards at the entrance to the command post went down, slumping to the ground as the assault force placed charges on the steel doors.

Taking cover to either side of the main door, they waited for the boom that echoed through the night. The ground shook slightly at the blast required to guarantee a breach through the thick, steel doors.

Troops surged through the entryway, and gunfire slammed some of them back as it struck their armor, or less often their arms, heads, or legs.

Men went down, injured and dead, but their comrades surged forward over them, firing on the run. Injured men rolled out of the way as they could, taking position behind whatever cover they could find.

As those still charging forward slowed their fire, those who had been injured and made it to cover took up the slack. The enemy guards were forced to keep their heads down until Boris's loyal soldiers crashed over them, killing or incapacitating them as quickly as a wave can destroy a sandcastle.

There were none of the hostages actually in the command post. That had been considered too risky, even by Viktor. After all, what would have happened to his plans if they had been listening in and managed to escape?

Finally, Boris reached the front of the charge. Troops were cut down by gunfire as they left the rooms they had been performing staff or communications duty from. An entire squad of half-dressed men was cut down by bursts of rifle fire as they turned out of what must have been a resting ready room.

Finally, he burst through a door from which the sounds of tables being overturned and other makeshift defenses being readied could be heard. Kicking down the thick wooden door, Boris burst into the room quickly enough to recognize Viktor as he attempted to flee through a door on the far side.

Time slowed as he saw the man responsible for all the pain death, destruction, and senseless waste he had seen in this campaign. Almost as if moving through syrup, his rifle rose to his shoulder, but everyone around him was moving slower. Taking careful aim, he fired a shot straight through the knee of this worm of the man.

A scream of agony ripped through the room. There were loud clatters as guns were dropped to the ground. Time sped up again for Boris, and he heard his enemy shouting through gritted teeth, "I surrender, damn it! I surrender!"

The others in the room raised their hands and backing up against the wall as Boris walked down the center of the room to his prey. When he reached Viktor, the coward was still face down on the floor, one hand under his body, the other splayed wide. Keeping his weapon trained on Viktor, Boris rolled him over with a booted foot. Boris half-expected the stupid, young fool to be holding a drawn pistol in his hidden hand.

When Viktor saw the cold anger in Boris's eyes, he blanched. In an almost panicked scream, he gibbered, "Try me in court, do whatever you want, just please…"

Whatever Viktor had been going to plead for, the world would never know for sure. Boris raised the muzzle of his rifle to the madman's face. The tired leader's face took on an expression of dispassionate justice. With no hesitation, he squeezed the trigger to send a three-round burst through Viktor's brain.

<<<>>>

With the capture of Viktor's command post, effective resistance along the perimeter slowly disintegrated. Fire teams and squads started surrendering as command devolved into conflicting orders from commanders who expected to be Viktor's successor. Reserve forces hunkered down in buildings intensifying the fortifications they had already put in place around their areas of responsibility.

Along the siege lines squads, fire teams, sometimes even single troopers, surrendered. Some few groups of troops rose up in defense of the civilians that Viktor had ordered be held hostage. Others simply threw them out of the areas they now controlled and settled in for smaller seizures. Food supplies had already been running low for the defenders of St. Petersburg when Boris had decapitated their command.

The result was just as inevitable. Boris was through wasting lives. Instead, he set up cordons around the remaining strong points and batted them into impotence with his artillery. Some few commanders from Viktor's forces tried to surrender for the sake of their own men's lives. Boris granted clemency to these as he could respect officers who cared more about their men's lives than their own.

Others tried to surrender for their own lives. Boris included commanders who had offered their own lives in exchange for their troop's lives as part of the negotiations teams. This caused several spontaneous mutinies to occur in large portions of the city.

After the mutinies, the now commanderless troops surrendered.

Still, maybe as many as a quarter of the strongpoints fought to the bitter end, to the death.

Not that they inflicted much death on Boris's forces. Now that he controlled the majority of the city's remaining food stores, and all its civilian population, he could afford to bombard them from a distance. With a civilian population free from retaliation, he had no qualms about simply battering whatever enemy forces remained from a distance. Within three weeks, the conquest of St. Petersburg was complete, and relief supplies were flooding into the city.

EPILOGUE

Alecta was still recovering from wounds in the battle. At the insistence of both Olaf and Boris, Paul had been used as a go-between to set up this summit. He was more sympathetic to Olaf's reasons than Boris's, to be honest. Olaf did not want to return, and Boris was being difficult, dictatorial, and somewhat ridiculous about it all.

The loss of an arm was inconvenient for Alecta, and time-consuming for Lilith to fix. More serious had been the two shells of buckshot that had been fired at point-blank almost directly into her face. If she had not been a Werebear, her chance of survival would have been between close to zero and absolute zero.

Even as a Werebear, she had taken weeks to be able to function normally. Her spine had suffered some minor damage. Even for nanites, that could be a slow repair.

In the end, Paul got a measure of revenge. He had organized the summit, but refused to mediate it. His advice had been to let Janna and Stasia negotiate the terms. Boris was not about to stand aside, and if he did not, neither would Olaf.

Boris approached the chosen meeting site with trepidation. It would be the first time he had seen his son Olaf in months. While Boris had been busy sorting out the division of the St. Petersburg region, Olaf had been busy organizing the partisan bands and population of the region encompassing a large section of Belarus and the North Ukraine into a functioning, governable entity.

Much to everyone's surprise, Olaf refused the offer of leading the region himself. Instead, he guaranteed to defend the realm with his life. "Father," Olaf said coolly as he saw Boris.

When Boris had first heard of his son's success, he had offered to integrate the region and people into his realm. Olaf had point blank refused. After they had been elected, so had the entire body of the two-house democracy that the new realm's constitution had formed.

Throughout history, both Belorussia and the Ukraine had been dominated by Russia. They wanted their free nationhood. Between the grain-rich plainlands of the Ukraine and the weapon stockpiles and improvisation and mechanical know-how of Belorussia, the region had a good chance at prosperity.

Perhaps it would have had a better chance at immediate and midterm survival as part of the realm Boris had built. But forgiveness, even for ancient mistakes, was not often in the spirit of peoples who had been recently, and historically, subjugated. Even an approach from a historical subjugator after a long time and global disaster, with the best in mind for the new realm, rankled the people too much for them to accept.

Even if a refusal of such unity endangered both parties. In this case, it only endangered the new realm.

"Son," Boris returned, respect clear both in his tone and his expression.

After the story of everything Olaf accomplished had spread through the militia units that had been designated as under his command, more than two-thirds of them transferred their direct loyalty to him. All the *Amazons* were amongst those so transferred. They were to form the core, along with some of the most experienced and a few of the youngest partisans, of the new defense force for the Ukraine regional government.

The father and son stared off at each other across the table. Neither would give in on this critical point. Olaf was refusing to return to Arkhangelsk, and Boris was standing firm on Olaf's status as heir. A status Boris felt required Olaf to live in New Romanovka.

To be fair, the twins just were not responsible enough to be designated heir. Now, Olaf had felt freedom from New Romanovka, and he had also found responsibility. One that bound him to the new realm. He had no desire to return.

Janna and Stasia had broken from the table to try and figure out a compromise that could be offered. In the end, Boris's demand was the one that had been folded. It was simply an unreasonable demand on his adult and more than adult son.

In return, the Ukrainian Republic would place a series of etheric communicators along the border and share any technology they found, especially plans that could upgrade existing oil-industry-based weapons systems and farm equipment to operate without diesel fuel.

Besides, as Janna had whispered to Boris before he agreed to the deal, it was unlikely that they would see any grandchildren if they forced Olaf to part with the determined Stasia. He was fascinated by her and would never forgive them for separating him from the unusual woman. Given how long Shifters tended to mourn the loss of a mate, it could be a century or more before he even started looking at women again, too.

After the agreement was reached, arrangements were made for etheric communications relays to be placed in locations of agreed strategic importance so there would always be a defense force on site. This would speed up the sharing of research from both sides. If Olaf were leaving New Romanovka for this fledgling Republic, then Boris would damned well make sure it had the best possible chance of survival.

FINIS

AUTHOR'S NOTES – PAUL C. MIDDLETON
JANUARY 3, 2017

I know I have been disappointing some of my many fans out there with how long this book has taken. It has been a year since I have published in the Kurtherian Universe. There are many reasons for this. I could have published earlier, but at the cost of giving you a much poorer book. I couldn't hurt you that way, nor would my pride let me.

For the first half of the year I was spending much of my time mastering my craft. Learning how to improve my writing in long stories and learning to write shorter ones (much of my production of which falls outside the Kurtherian Universe.)

Every so often I've paused and wished honing writing skills was as easy, or at least straightforward, as sharpening a blade. It isn't. However I am still finding writing fun. That is always a plus for something you hope will make up all your income eventually

I also had several bouts of illness and a Major Depressive Episode. (I cover the MDE in a short autobiographical piece, the Black Dog and when it Bites, in the *Against the Tide* Anthology that will be released in January)

I found this book hard to write well. To make it the best book

I could for you, my fans. But I got there in the end. At least I hope I did.

I think I got the balance right for the Military fiction genre it is mainly aimed at.

The final judgement, of course, lays at the feet of you, my fans. I have improved my art massively over the year I feel.

It also caused me to rework Evacuation, which at the time of this publication I hope has been updated (cleaned, cleared and some pure Janna sections added to improve the depth of her character.)

I hope you enjoy it and you decide to give it positive reviews.

Oh, and that you look at my other works, They are as good, or better, depending on your genre preferences.

Paul C Middleton

AUTHOR'S NOTES – MICHAEL ANDERLE
JANUARY 4, 2017

Whoop!

First, let me thank you for not only reading this story, but ALSO reading through our author notes as well.

Paul had a HELL of a 2017, and I hope that 2018 treats him a lot better personally with his health. We both want to thank you for not only supporting him, but encouraging him through the tough times and ever-so-patiently waiting as we get this book out to you at the 'right' time.

Boris and his family are fighting the good fight and working together to protect those they love, and yet allowing them to grow in tough times.

You can't always protect those you love.

For myself, I have two young men that have gone to college, and I am now spending some time with them as they transition between their first and second semester. It's a challenge to not 'protect' them from themselves, at times.

However, I'm learning that we have to let our children make their mistakes, and pay for their mistakes, or they will likely continue to make them far into their future.

Hurting themselves over and over again.

Often, failure (and suffering due to the failure) is the quickest route to learning NOT to do the shortcuts in life.

Or, at least it is the first of a multitude of times that life teaches us a lesson as it chips away at our stubbornness. Occasionally, we beat life and win.

Typically, life beats us.

This is a NEW YEAR, and we are leaving behind the crap that happened in 2017 (to the best of our abilities) and accepting all the cool stuff (like you!) that 2018 is bringing.

May you and your loved ones have a fun, and fantastic year.

Ad Aeternitatem,
Michael

Mongrelverse Series

Breed Matters

- Book 1 – A Mongrel's Curse
- Book 2 – Mongrel's Tooth and Consequence (2nd Quarter 2017)

Face The Music

- Book 1 – WereEagles Fear to Tread
- Book 2 – A Mongrel, A Bard and Witches, Oh My!

Mother of Monsters

- Book 1 – Cursed Mother (1st Quarter 2017)
- Book 2 – Forsaking Motherhood (2nd Quarter 2017)
- Book 3 – Mother Remade (2nd Quarter 2017)

Misc. Shorts

- A Simple Trip
- Guarding An Imp (published in Flight of the Phoenix Anthology)

Betrayed by Faith

- Book 1 – Paladin
- Book 2 - A-Viking
- Book 3 – Myrmidon (3rd Quarter 2017)

The Boris Chronicles (Kurtherian Universe, With Michael Anderle)

- Book 1 – Evacuation
- Book 2 - Retaliation
- Book 3 - Revelations
- Book 4 – Title pending (2nd Quarter 2017)

Short Story Contributions to Anthologies

- Inanna's Circle Game, Volume 4 (edited by Kat Lind)
- The Expanding Universe, Volume 1 (edited by Craig Martelle)

These can be found and will be published on Paul C Middleton's Author page.

WANT MORE PAUL C MIDDLETON?

Join Paul's Email List here: http://eepurl.com/bZxFvD

Join Paul's Facebook Group Here: https://www.facebook. com/Betrayed-by-Faith-1110766018944080/